"Once you leave Start," continued the Teacher, "the danger is constant. There's no instant for relaxation, no time to breathe freely. Death is there beside you at all times, waiting eagerly for you to let down your guard for even the tiniest instant.

"Yes, there are those who become too afraid to go out. They are those who live long enough to know fear! The only creatures on the face of this planet that are not afraid are the dead!"

"Do those who become afraid ever go back out again?" Seeker asked gently.

"Oh, yes, mostly."

"What happens to those that don't?"

"They just waste away." The Teacher shot a sidelong glance up at Seeker. "Though if you want my opinion, I think it's Labyrinth that kills them. The planet finds a way into their minds, and then it kills them slowly, but just as surely as if they walked its surface . . ."

LABYRINTH

DENNIS SCHMIDT

ACE BOOKS, NEW YORK

All Heidegger quotes from *Being and Time*:
Introduction, translated by J. Stambaugh,
in collaboration with J. G. Gray, and
D. F. Krell in *Martin Heidegger Basic Writings*.
Reprinted by permission of Harper & Row, Publishers, Inc.

LABYRINTH

An Ace Book / published by arrangement with
the author

PRINTING HISTORY
Ace edition / October 1989

ISBN: 0-441-69337-7

10 9 8 7 6 5 4 3 2 1

This book is dedicated to S.K. and M.H. with my sincerest apologies

First
Immediacy

. . . the highest and most beautiful things in life are not to be heard about, nor read about, nor seen, but, if one will, may be lived.

Soren Kierkegaard

Swift stood at the top of the ridge, poised for instant motion. Its comb was fully extended, glowing bright red, warning off any killbirds that might be cruising the skies. Every hair was extended to its fullest, testing and judging the fitful breezes of early morning. The flap of skin that covered the nostrils was raised to suck in great gulps of air, seeking telltale scents. Large ears had unfolded to their full size and scanned to and fro to pick up the tiniest sounds. Two eyes, almost as keen as those of a glidewing, swept the grassy plain in every direction as the head swiveled back and forth. Even the transparent membrane that covered them during the chase to protect them from the wind was retracted so that as much of the dim early light as possible could be gathered.

The plain swept off toward the horizon in a series of gentle undulations. Swift's viewpoint was the best for many miles. From it, the slightest motion of even the smallest creature could be seen, heard, or smelled. The ridge was an aberration, a sudden upthrust in a land of gentle swellings. Swift had discovered it several seasons ago and instantly had recognized its value as a vantage point for seeking game.

As far as Swift knew, it was the only Chaser to have ventured this far east this early in the White Grass Season. The white flowers that gave the time its name still dotted the plain, hiding just beneath the tops of the grass. Their light fragrance hung in the air, drifting with the breezes. Most of the larger grasseaters arrived only after the blossoms were gone, for they had a bitter taste the creatures appeared to dislike. Swift knew of the taste because it had nibbled on them experimentally one time during the previous blossoming season. Since the grasseaters didn't like the flowers, the other Chasers reasoned, there would be no game in this part of the plain until the flowers were gone.

Swift knew differently. True, *most* of the grasseaters didn't like the flowers, but the tiny hoppers didn't seem to mind them, and one type of springrunner appeared to seek them out. Both were very small and swift, so most of the other Chasers didn't think it worthwhile to hunt them. Swift, though, found the challenge irresistible. And what was more, several of its favorite Catchers took especial pleasure in the almost impossible task of catching the little creatures when Swift chased them by.

Finesse, Swift thought, that's what it's all about. Some Chasers were happy to chase any old thing to the Catchers. In fact, the slower and dopier the game, the better as far as they were concerned. Big lumbering beasts like the stumpers or the heavyhorns were what *those* kinds of Chasers sought out. And their Catchers were just as lazy as they were—only grabbing those animals that virtually ran them over!

Not so, Swift. Swift prided itself on always seeking out the toughest prey, the small, the fast, the tricky. In fact, Swift thought with a small mirthful snort, I'm the only Chaser that's ever driven a poisontooth! Swift opened its mouth, and the high-pitched growl that indicated amusement among its species welled out of its chest. Ah! Ah! How even the strongest and best of the Catchers had scattered when they'd seen that poisontooth bearing down on them! Swift had literally hovered around it, darting from side to side, pushing it, nipping and dodging at the same time, worrying the dangerous beast, driving it at top speed, staying just out of its reach. No one had been too sure who was chasing whom until Swift had led it straight to Crusharm, a Catcher Swift particularly disliked. With a roar of fear, Crusharm had fallen over backwards in its efforts to escape! How Swift had laughed to see that! Then

Swift had brought the poisontooth back around again to Dreadclaw, a Catcher as much given to the game as Swift was. Dreadclaw had darted in just as the poisontooth was passing and had ripped one of its legs off as it sped by. Two more passes, two more legs, and the thing was slowing down. Then Dreadclaw had made its kill. Of course the thing hadn't been edible, and both Dreadclaw and Swift had been criticized for frivolity by the Nurturers, but it had been worth it. Their whole section of the plain had been humming with talk of the exploit from the Yellow Sun Season until the Tall Flower Season.

Swift rose to its toes, stretching out its long limbs, ruffling its honey-colored fur. It stood about six feet, or one stride, tall, about average for Chasers. Swift resembled nothing so much as a bipedal cheetah with extra-long legs and tiny arms. The legs resembled those of an ostrich, but covered with more flesh and muscle. They were hairless and ended in paws that bore retractable claws.

The muzzle was more pointed than that of a cheetah, and the head was narrower with a crest on top. The crest folded flat against the skull for running, but when Swift was standing still it rose up to warn off killbirds. The eyes were larger than those of a cheetah and placed in the curved front of the face to give Swift excellent depth perception. A large flap that could be opened and closed at will served to cover the nose opening. The mouth was small and oval, filled with tiny but sharp teeth. At the sides of Swift's head, just behind the eyes, were two large ears that moved back and forth, gathering sounds from every direction. They folded down into grooves when Swift was running. Once the game was on the run, Swift depended entirely on its eyesight for the chase.

On Swift's back, right between the shoulder blades, were six lumps each about two inches wide by four long. These were the sacks that held Swift's protoeggs. Every Chaser developed six protoeggs upon reaching maturity. One of Swift's had already been harvested by a Catcher, and for all Swift knew had already been implanted in the birthing pouch of a Nurturer. Still five to go, Swift reminded itself with a slight shudder. Five. But Swift knew that another was rapidly maturing. The itch had been growing day by day. Soon a Catcher would notice and . . . No! Swift dragged its mind away from the thought. *I still have many seasons of running the plains* until . . . Swift shook its head as if trying to dislodge an unpleasant idea. Don't worry about it now, Swift ordered itself. Concentrate on finding game.

Swift stretched again. Ah, but it was good to be the fastest Chaser on the plain! The joy of running, of the wind in its hair, of the grass swishing by, the feel of the ground as each foot came down, just for an instant, just long enough to impart forward momentum without creating too much friction. Ah, that was sheer delight! And when the sun was shining brightly and light yellow clouds flecked the sky, spattering their wispy shadows across the surface of the plain . . . ah, then it was utter glory to be running down the fastest game that could be found. The very idea of becoming slow and thick and powerful . . . Stop it! Swift commanded itself. Why am I so morbid on such a wonderful day? it wondered. It must be because I haven't chased in several days, such was my haste to get out here before the others arrived. Once I'm running again, I'll be fine. I'll . . .

A movement high in the sky caught Swift's attention. A killbird? No, hardly. It was much too high for a killbird. Plus, the shape was all wrong. Swift narrowed its eyes for a better look. The Chaser gave a sudden growl of pleased recognition. A glidewing! How Swift loved glidewings! They soared so effortlessly, hanging in the air, sweeping round and round in great spirals, diving with sudden speed, then swooping unexpectedly back into the depths of the sky. What incredible freedom of movement, Swift thought as it gazed up at the wheeling form of the glidewing. It moves in any direction with greater speed and ease than even the swiftest Chaser on the plain.

Swift growled softly with pleasure. Watching glidewings always gave Swift a warm, happy feeling. The other Chasers had snarled with derision when Swift had mentioned its interest in the flying creatures. No value as game, they had chided. Can't chase a glidewing, they had declared. Some Catchers had rumbled their agreement. But Dreadclaw had smiled gently and nodded to Swift with understanding in those deepset Catcher eyes. Swift more than half suspected that long ago Dreadclaw had gazed up at glidewings itself. Long ago.

How I would love to be a glidewing! the Chaser thought with sudden enthusiasm. Then, rather than just skimming along the tops of the grass, never quite getting off the ground, I could soar up into the clouds and never stop! What joy! What joy! What . . .

Ear, nose, and eye simultaneously sensed a slight movement off to the left. Swift swiveled its head in that direction and stared and sniffed and listened. Yes! It was a springdasher, one of the very fastest beasts alive! Swift knew of no Chaser that had ever managed to drive one to a Catcher. Nor was there really much reason to. The creature had hardly any meat on it. It was mostly legs, heart, and lungs. Plus keen eyes and very large, sensitive ears that heard even the slightest footfall. Why chase such impossible, useless game? Because! Swift challenged itself. Because!

The springdasher was actually nibbling at the flowers! Of course, Swift realized, that makes sense. The flowers are very bitter because they are a very concentrated form of the same food stuff that is in the grass. A creature like the springdasher that burns up so much energy needs to gather a lot of energy as efficiently as possible. Hence it had managed somehow to get used to the bitterness.

Swift had two choices. First, it could take out after the springdasher right away and hope to run it down. That didn't seem such a good idea. The creature was perhaps a hundred full strides away. Even if Swift could cover half the distance before the little beast became aware of the Chaser (a highly unlikely thing, given the springdasher's keen senses), it was doubtful Swift could make up the difference in time to turn the springdasher and head it in the right direction.

The second choice wasn't much better. It was to stay put, motionless, hoping the creature would move closer. Even ten strides would make all the difference in the world. But the odds were against the springdasher moving in the right direction. It could just as easily move away. Besides, Swift admitted, quivering slightly in anticipation, I want to run, not stand around! I'm a Chaser! The best ever!

Swift whooped and exploded from the ridgetop in the direction of the springdasher. Its legs pumped so swiftly they were a blur of motion. The springdasher was startled by the whoop and didn't react for at least seven of Swift's strides. Then it was in motion too, its six legs propelling it across the plain with a speed that dazzled the eye.

Twice before Swift had chased springdashers. Both times the creatures had outdistanced the Chaser after a fairly short run. And both times the other Chasers had called Swift a fool for wasting energy and time on such useless game.

But on both occasions Swift had noticed something about the springdashers. The creatures were incredibly fast, true, but they ran in a pattern! They ran a long arc that curved back toward their starting place. The last two times Swift had followed the springdashers along the curve of the arc. This time it would be different.

Once Swift saw which way the arc was bending, it cut across the arc on an interception course. Swift doubted the tactic would work perfectly. Surely the springdasher would see it coming from the side and veer off. But it would probably veer into a new arc and Swift could then cut across that one. Eventually one of three things would happen. The springdasher would be caught on one of the arcs. The springdasher would become confused and do something different, something that might give Swift a chance to catch it. The springdasher would leave Swift in its dust. The last seemed most likely. But I really don't care, Swift admitted to itself with a grin that looked more like a snarl. I'm running! I'm flying! I'm Swift!

The springdasher saw Swift approaching from behind and to the side. Its astonishment was clear even to the Chaser. It threw a quick glance behind it and saw that the creature it thought was there was gone. Am I a second Chaser? Swift asked the little beast with a growl. Heh? Or the first where you didn't expect it?

The little creature lost a good two strides to indecision, then took off suddenly and with furious intensity in a new direction. Swift stayed on its trail long enough to ascertain the direction the arc curved in and cut across it.

For a second time, the springdasher discovered the Chaser where it shouldn't be. This time, however, it didn't even hesitate. It simply poured on speed and ran at an angle to its former trajectory. Swift followed and quickly realized the little creature was no longer running in an arc. It was hightailing it across the plain in a dead straight line.

As luck would have it, the direction the springdasher had chosen was the opposite of where Swift wanted to head it. And now there would be no way to turn it again. All the Chaser could do was follow in its wake.

At that point any sensible Chaser would have broken off the pursuit. Of course, any sensible Chaser wouldn't be chasing a springdasher in the first place, Swift reminded itself with a growly chuckle. Which just proves I'm not a sensible Chaser!

Swift leaned forward slightly and opened up all its power. Its legs pumped faster and faster, taking longer and longer strides that ate up the plain. The Chaser raised its noseflap and flared it out to form a scoop to force more air into its lungs. Its mouth opened wide for the same purpose. Every hair was pulled tightly against its skin to offer as little wind resistance as possible.

It felt as if Swift was flying. An exhilaration filled its chest and mind and it called out in a high, whistling growl of sheer joy. The sun was finally rising, and Swift was swooping across the plain to meet it.

The springdasher and the Chaser ran as if they were one beast. Neither gained nor lost an inch to the other. They moved, no, flew across the white blossoms in total unity. Swift heard the springdasher squealing in a delight that matched its own. It was no longer a question of chaser and chased. They were running *with* each other. No greater happiness existed for a Chaser.

The sun climbed high and higher into the sky. The land began to rise, gently at first, but more steeply as they went. Then, in the distance, so far off it was almost a suggestion rather than a real perception, Swift saw something that made it slow down and finally stop and gaze in wonder. Forgotten, the springdasher scurried well beyond range, then stopped and looked back almost wistfully at the Chaser.

Swift didn't even notice. Its eyes were totally absorbed with the vision that filled them. There at the very edge of sight, the land towered up and up into the sky until it disappeared into the yellow clouds themselves. Up—the land went up, not out! The plain stood on its end and reached for the sky!

For a long time Swift stood and stared, fascinated and confounded by the sight. Never before had the Chaser seen the plain act that way. Always and always it just ran on, gently rolling, rising occasionally to a ridge, then dropping back down and running out toward the horizon. But there, far, far off toward where the sun rose, it stood on its end and climbed into the sky! How could such a thing be? No Nurturer had ever told Swift of such a thing, not even Fairsayer, the Litter Teacher. Swift was certain no other Chaser had ever seen it either, or they would have bragged about it. But then, that was understandable, for no Chaser Swift knew of had ever come into this part of the plain before. Nor had any of them ever chased a springdasher the way Swift had!

Swift gave a small roar of pride. I have chased springdashers and seen the plain rise into the sky! Surely I am the greatest Chaser ever to exist!

The Chaser looked up at the sun. It was past the halfway point. Swift had spent all morning chasing the springdasher and now would have to spend the rest of the day running hard to get back to the pack before dark fell.

When I get back, Swift thought as it turned and began to follow the sun once again, but now in the opposite direction, the other Chasers will laugh at me. They'll say I'm a fool and a time-waster, going after springdashers and other useless game. If there are any Catchers around, they'll grumble and snarl at me, threatening me with their long claws and sharp teeth, saying I'm a burden to the pack, eating and not providing.

But then I'll start to tell them of the run and how I almost flew across the plain. I'll talk of how I almost fooled the springdasher and how we ran as companions. I'll show them the beauty of the white flowers and the rising sun and the clouds and the wonder of the plain rising into the sky.

And they'll fall silent. The Catchers will wipe their eyes with their massive paws and think of how it once was. The Chasers will dream of flying and running and they will smile and know what I felt.

And none of them will call me fool any longer.

Every questioning is a seeking. Every seeking takes its direction beforehand from what is sought.

Martin Heidegger

I.

The ship was old, cluttered, and in a poor state of repair. Since it had to do the double duty of traversing open space and making falls on the surfaces of planets too primitive to have orbiting terminals and shuttles, it had none of the open, free design of ships that never suffered the stresses of friction and gravity, nor did it possess the sleek grace of ships which sliced through atmosphere. In other words, it was exactly the kind of ugly old tub that always makes the odd runs, the trips to out-of-the-way places where almost no one ever wants to go. Three falls had been scheduled. Two had already been made. The last was only a few hours away.

There were six passengers, which was somewhat surprising, since there were many runs when no one but the crew was aboard. Six all at once, and all going to the last stop; well, it was just unusual, that's all.

Four of the passengers were crammed together in the tiny compartment that went by the euphemistic name of Ship's Commons. It contained a broken tape viewer, a drink vendor which was out of everything interesting, several decrepit chairs in various shapes, and a rather battered round table that the crew sometimes used for playing cards.

The four were an odd lot, to be as polite as possible about it.

One, seated at the table, was dressed in a deeply cowled robe of a nasty, mustardy yellow. The robe swept to the floor and showed not one inch of the creature's flesh, assuming it had any, and gave only vague hints as to its shape. Where there should have been a face peering from the folds of the hood, there was a bland mask of some white substance with two slits apparently cut so the creature could see. The sleeves of the robe, which started strangely far below the shoulder, were long and full and showed nothing of the arms, if arms there were, that lurked within them.

Seated, or rather crouching, on a chair directly across from the hooded figure was a small, brownish-red saurian. The creature had a narrow head that came to a short, narrow snout. Two large, green eyes were mounted on either side of the head in bulging sockets that allowed them to swivel through more than one hundred eighty degrees. Indeed, they never seemed to stop swiveling and darted nervously in every direction. The body was slender and made for speed and evasion. It had a distinctly slippery look, and when the creature moved, it bent in unexpected places, making it appear as though it had no joints. It wore no clothing except for a harness about its middle. An array of bizarre instruments or fetishes or weapons or somethings hung from the harness.

A third being, dressed in a nondescript brown robe, sat on a chair that was turned to face a peeling bulkhead. It was short and simian in appearance. Its bandy legs were tucked up under it, and its long arms were folded calmly in its lap. Its face was fixed in a perpetual grin by a pair of thick lips that curved up at the ends. It had no nose to speak of. The eyes were large and soft and placed in the front of its head. It was gazing fixedly at the peeling paint of the wall as if it was reading messages of profound importance there.

The final figure in the room was a good bit taller and even odder than the other three. It resembled nothing so much as a six-foot-tall bumblebee that had failed to grow wings and lacked one pair of legs. Its face was round and contained two very large compound eyes and a beaklike protuberance from which a buzzing, humming sound ceaselessly issued forth. The creature appeared to be extremely uncomfortable in the tiny room. It stood in a corner and shifted anxiously from one foot to the other, back and forth, back and forth.

The hooded creature was the only one that really seemed to be interested in conversation. It kept addressing comments to the other three, even when they weren't listening or replying. Its voice was dull and monotonous. It spoke Federation Common with a perfect, scholarly diction and uttered each word with a mathematical precision that utterly lacked personality.

There was a movement at the door to the room and all eyes, except for the simian's which stayed glued to the wall, turned to see who was about to enter. A large, honey-colored, bearlike being stepped into the room. It was a few inches less than six feet in height and nearly as wide. Yet despite its bulk, it moved with smooth grace. The face contained two liquid brown eyes, a short snout tipped with a black nose, and a tooth-filled mouth. A red comb rose briefly on the top of its head as it noticed the others in the room. Its arms were long and powerful, but ended in fingers rather than claws. The body was shaped like a barrel and had six bulges in two rows of three each, low on the front. Two stout, sturdy legs held it above the ship's deck. "I am Seeker," it announced to the others in passable Federation Common. "I am going to Labyrinth."

"This unit surmises as much," said the hooded figure. "It is quite evident that all the passengers still aboard this ship are destined for fall on Labyrinth since that is the last stop for this run. However, the question this unit wishes to pose for consideration is why any of the passengers should wish to fall on Labyrinth. Surely they are all acquainted with the odds. The latest data, available from the Federation files as of two cycles ago, indicates that the mortality rate now exceeds ninety-three percent. That means that for every hundred units that make fall on the planet, fewer than seven will survive. This unit assumes that the other passengers are aware of these statistics and cannot image why, if they are truly sapient beings, they would wish to go to Labyrinth."

"And yet," hissed the sibilant voice of the small saurian, "you go yourssself, no?"

"The surmise is correct, as far as it goes," the robed one replied. "But the situation is not similar for this unit and other creatures. This unit is a portion of a race of superior sentience. Labyrinth holds no fears for this unit. It cannot fail."

The ursoid growled for attention. "I said I am called Seeker.

My race, whether of superior sentience or not, has the superior courtesy of exchanging names when offered. Only enemies fail to exchange names." It swiveled its head around the room and glared at each of the others. "Now. I am called Seeker."

"I . . . um . . . well . . . yesss. The nearessst thing in Federation Common to my name isss Darkhider," replied the saurian, cringing slightly beneath the gaze of Seeker. Seeker nodded pleasantly and turned to look at the hooded creature.

"This unit has no designation that translates into Federation Common. There is no need for individual unit designation. Therefore, my race . . ."

"Of superior sentience, no doubt," Seeker snorted drily. "No name, eh? Then I'll give you one. Hmmmmm. How does 'Thisunit' sound to you, Darkhider?"

Darkhider hissed in approval. "Ah, yesss! Very appropriate, though Longtalker might alssso do."

Seeker considered for a moment. "No, Thisunit is better. More neutral. Someone named Longtalker might actually be worth listening to. We haven't established that fact about Thisunit yet." The ursoid turned to the creature standing in the corner. "And you, are you called Hummer or something like that?"

"Something like that," came a soft, buzzing reply. "My name is H*mb*l," it said, pronouncing the word in a way that made it seem a humming with a plosive in the middle and ending with a drawn-out sigh. "If you cannot pronounce that, the closest meaning in Federation Common would be . . ." It paused, ruminating. "Ah . . . yes, it would be 'One Who Dances With Swirls.' "

Seeker tried several times to pronounce the name and decided it had it close enough. "Very well, I vote for H*mb*l. I like it. It suits you. Now," Seeker continued as it stepped fully into the room, "that leaves only the wall watcher. Are you awake over there?"

A sigh came from the being in the brown robe. Its long arms came out of its lap, reached down and braced firmly against the floor, and then lifted up the chair and its body, spun it around to face the others and let it back down. Finished, the arms folded neatly into the lap. It was then that they all noticed the insignia on the front of the creature's robe. Stitched in gold just below the left shoulder was a small maze.

The other four all sucked in their breath in surprise. Seeker bowed low. "Pardon. I had no idea you were *returning* to Labyrinth, Father."

"Yes, I'm returning to Labyrinth, and don't call me 'Father.'" There was a slight hint of suppressed laughter in the voice. "My species and yours aren't even remotely related, and I never met your mother, I assure you." Seeker looked confused and stepped back. "Calm yourself, good heavens, be calm! I'm from Labyrinth but I'm hardly as dangerous as the planet! I live mostly at Start and teach fools such as yourself who take it into their heads to become Questioners."

"You are a Teacher?" asked the saurian. It was bobbing its head up and down with respect.

The Teacher pulled its lips back from yellowed teeth in a laugh. "You make it sound holy! Yes, I'm a Teacher. My name is Longarm, for obvious reasons."

"But a Teacher . . ." said Thisunit, somehow managing to get wonder into its dull voice.

"Oh, grubs and sandbobbers, will all of you stop it!? All a Teacher does is talk to the few who make it past the first months on Labyrinth and try to help them understand what's going on. And believe me, it takes some understanding!"

"Then you have walked on Labyrinth?" Seeker asked with a quick intake of breath.

"Walked, run, crawled, jumped, scrambled, fled, hid, you name it! I've even slithered through mud on my belly like a snake!"

"All the way to Sanctuary?"

Longarm paused thoughtfully. "Ah, now *that* I can't tell you, can I? For that would be declaring myself a Questioner, and you know that Questioners aren't allowed to do that in the flesh, don't you? Well, you should."

"If you *are* a Questioner," H*mb*l said, buzzing excitedly, "you must be on your way back from a mission and . . ."

The Teacher laughed again and shook its shaggy head in mild exasperation. "I didn't say I *am* a Questioner! Indeed, there's a very good reason to suspect that I am *not*. After all, Questioners don't come back from missions in broken-down old commercial tramps. They come back, if and when they come back at all, in their own probe ships. I told you, I'm a

Teacher. You'll probably be seeing more of me at Start than you wish to."

"This unit will not remain at Start for long. It will proceed immediately to Sanctuary," droned the robed figure.

"'Immediately'?" Seeker snorted derisively. "Pretty sure of yourself, aren't you?"

A vague shrug moved the robe's fabric. "It is self-evident. This unit cannot fail."

Darkhider hissed. "How can that be?"

"It is the logical conclusion to be drawn from the available facts. Labyrinth is a sentient being. A sentient planet. It seeks to kill all beings of lesser sentience that exist, or try to exist, on its surface. A creature of higher sentience, such as this unit, will be able to outreason it with ease and avoid its traps and stratagems. Therefore, this unit will have no trouble in going directly to Sanctuary."

"Bah!" thundered a new voice from the door. "Stupidity!" They all turned to view a huge creature that resembled a cross between an elephant and a lion. Its legs were round and powerful, ending in feet like those of an elephant. Its body was barrellike and muscular, covered with a dark, close fur. Two well-muscled arms ended in hands of six fingers, each tipped with a razor-sharp, retractable claw. The neck was thick and blended directly into a huge, rounded head. Large mobile ears stuck out from the sides of the head and moved slowly back and forth as if a gentle breeze was softly blowing them. Two small, keen eyes were placed on either side of a long snout that could plainly sniff out the slightest trace of an enemy. The mouth was a grim slash just beneath the nose and was filled with many sharp and pointed teeth.

The creature wore the harness and insignia of the Emperor's Elite Guard. There had been no Emperor and no Guard for many generations, but in certain families of professional soldiers, the uniform was passed down from generation to generation. What they were all gazing at with wonder was an example of just such a creature. It was from a heavy-gravity planet much closer to the Center, and its race had formed the core of the armies of the Empire when long ago such a thing had been dared. The Empire had ended in miserable failure. An empire was impossible among the stars, the distances being too long and the costs of traversing them too great. But this race, known as the Furmorians after their planet, still maintained the military disciplines of the Empire and often hired out as mercenary soldiers on other worlds.

"I am Bilrog of the Mighty Arms," the Furmorian said, glaring around at all of them with a truculent expression. It settled its gaze on the hooded figure. "Are you expecting to use logic against Labyrinth?"

"Indeed," Thisunit replied weakly.

"Rubbish!" Bilrog thundered. "Labyrinth is a killer, and killers only understand one thing . . . brute power! I am the mightiest warrior in all the worlds of the Federation and the first of my race to come to Labyrinth." Bilrog looked around at them triumphantly. "You may all follow me. I will battle Labyrinth and subdue it. I will fight my way to Sanctuary."

"You . . . you'll fight a *planet*?" Darkhider hissed in astonishment.

"Yes! Fight and smash and conquer!"

Darkhider looked disturbed. "Dear me, no, no, that'sss not for Darkhider. No, Darkhider goesss sssoftly, quietly, hiding, ssslipping by without being ssseen. Never fightsss, oh, no. Run, hide, avoid, that'sss the only way to sssurvive. Yesss, that'sss it. Darkhider hasss no teeth or clawsss, no massssive armsss or quick weaponsss."

Bilrog scowled with scorn at the saurian. "A race of cowardly lizards! The Empire would have crushed you in a day. Only those who stand up and fight Labyrinth have any hope of survival!"

H*mb*l was clearly agitated and was shifting back and forth more rapidly than ever. "No, no," H*mb*l buzzed in consternation. "You don't understand. You don't have to *fight* Laybrinth. You just have to *dance* it."

Seeker looked at H*mb*l with interest. "I've never heard that phrase before, 'to dance Labyrinth.' What does it mean?"

H*mb*l stopped shifting back and forth for a moment and said, "There is nothing I can say. It is something one does. There is no logic to it," H*mb*l said with an apologetic nod to Thisunit, "and it takes no warrior's strength," with a glance at Bilrog, "nor even a cautious avoidance," throwing a sidelong glance at Darkhider. "It is simply listening to Labyrinth, hearing its music and moving with it."

"Musssic?" Darkhider asked. "I've never heard that Labyrinth playsss any musssic. You mussst be wrong."

"Well," H*mb*l said softly as if becoming confused, "not *really* music. That's just my way of explaining it. The important thing is that you mustn't hate or fear Labyrinth. It isn't your enemy. It's . . . it's your . . . dance partner. I can't . . ."

"Not fear Labyrinth? Not our enemy?" Darkhider hissed in angry surprise. "By the Original Egg, the planet killsss ninety-three out of every hundred beingsss that ssset foot or paw or hoof or tentacle or whatever on it and you sssay it is our dansssse partner? You mussst be an idiot! I've dansssed every year in the Time of the Egg and never had a partner that tried to kill me!"

"An idiot, a fool," muttered the hooded figure in agreement.

"Worse yet," Bilrog chimed in with a sneer and a hostile glare in H*mb*l's direction, "a weak, cowardly fool!"

Longarm heaved a huge sigh and turned itself back toward the bulkhead. In an instant, the creature was once again deeply engrossed in the patterns made by the peeling paint.

Seeker looked around at the others and shook a shaggy head in mild exasperation. Then it turned and shuffled over to H*mb*l and began to murmur softly growling questions to the strange creature as it started to shift back and forth from one leg to the other once more.

"But surely," Thisunit addressed Bilrog again, "you do not believe that physical force is superior to reason? It can clearly be proven that in solving a problem such as this, reason is the only method which . . ."

The Furmorian took two steps toward Thisunit and held a clawed hand beneath its mask. "How will you reason with death when it is this close to you?" Bilrog growled viciously.

Before anybody could say or do anything, a bored voice came over the ship's intercom. "All passengers immediately return to landing berths. Fall to Labyrinth begins in three minutes."

Without another look at each other, the six filed from the Ship's Common and went to their staterooms for landing.

II.

The six of them stood on a plain oval slab of concretelike material and gazed about them. The few pieces of baggage they had brought were piled next to them in a tumbled heap. Behind was the ship they had come in and the ramp they had walked down. In the far distance, they could see mountains rising purple toward a deep blue sky. Bluish wisps of cloud drifted overhead. A hot, blue-white sun was about to set to their left.

Closer, but still a good mile or so away, they could perceive a cluster of rough buildings that clung to a hillside. Even at this distance, they appeared run-down and unimpressive. Between the landing oval and the "town," a dusty path stretched off in a straight line.

Bilrog scowled and grunted angrily. "Not even a damn terminal! And not a soul around to greet us!"

Longarm chuckled. "That's because no one knows or cares that you've come. By the Primordial Tree, friend, if you can't find your way to town by that path, you're not fit to venture onto the surface of your own world, much less Labyrinth!"

"I take it this is Start?" Seeker asked drily.

"This," the Teacher replied, "is the landing oval. That"—a long arm rose and pointed in the direction of the cluster of buildings—"is Start. Although all this land, from the oval to the town, is fairly safe, if you stray far from the path you might not make it to Start. Labyrinth isn't usually too vicious in this area, but one can never afford to take anything for granted on this planet."

"No one isss coming to greet usss?" Darkhider asked in dismay. "We are jussst to make our own way? What might have happened if you had not been with usss, Longarm? We might have perissshed through ignorance!"

Longarm shrugged. "It happens all the time. Pretenders land and just wander off in confusion. Very few of them last more than an hour or two."

"But that is an illogical waste of material," Thisunit complained. "It would be far more reasonable, if there is a shortage of personnel, to post warnings and instructions so that . . ."

"Cease with all this babble of logic," Bilrog snarled with a glare at Thisunit. The huge warrior turned to the Teacher and said, "You mentioned 'Pretenders.' What's a 'Pretender'?"

"You are," Longarm chuckled. "Anyone on Labyrinth who isn't a Teacher or a Novice or a Questioner is called a Pretender. But come, we're standing here talking and the sun is setting. Even Start isn't completely safe at night. I'll lead you all to the town so you can find quarters. I'm afraid it's too late to get an evening meal. But you were all probably clever and resourceful enough to bring food along for the ship's journey, since ship food is close to inedible no matter what your species. If not, well, a night of hunger may teach you an important lesson, it might indeed. Tomorrow you can begin. Yes, tomorrow will be soon enough. Though perhaps you'll have a chance to meet some other Pretenders tonight and bedevil them with your questions. Hmmmm. That is, if there are any Pretenders left in Start." Without waiting for them, Longarm picked up a sack it had brought from the ship and slung it over its back. Then, holding the sack with one hand, it began to shamble forward with a rolling, three-legged gait, using its free arm and its two bandy legs.

Seeker walked along next to Longarm. "Why did you say 'if' there are any Pretenders in Start?"

Longarm shrugged. "They may all be dead by now. Or they may all be out trying to cross Labyrinth to get to Sanctuary. Pretenders only stay in Start when they're too afraid to go out or when they're resting and recuperating between attempts."

"Too afraid to go out?" Bilrog thundered. "How can that be? Am I surrounded with cowards and idiots?"

Longarm stopped and spun around to face the giant creature. "Don't judge too swiftly, warrior! Many brave creatures have been frightened by Labyrinth! The only idiots here are those stupid enough *not* to be afraid." Bilrog blinked in surprise and just stared openmouthed at the Teacher.

"Labyrinth is deadly, make no mistake about that," Longarm continued after a pause. "It's more deadly than anything you've ever experienced. It can get inside your mind and soul and discover those things which most horrify you. It can delve deep into you and find those secret places where primitive fear lurks and gibbers. And then it can make those things real and place them in your path. Once you leave Start, the danger is constant. There's no instant for relaxation, no time to breathe freely. Death is there beside you at all times, waiting eagerly for you to let down your guard for even the tiniest instant.

"Yes, Bilrog, there are those who become too afraid to go out. Shall I tell you who they are? Very well. They are those who live long enough to know fear! The only creatures on the face of this planet that are not afraid are the dead! Or the foolish! And very swiftly the latter will become the former." The Teacher swung around again, giving Bilrog and the others its back, and began to shuffle off toward the town once more.

"Do those who become afraid ever go back out again?" Seeker asked gently.

"Oh, yes, mostly," Longarm replied offhandedly. "Most get their fear under control and go back out."

"You say 'most.' What happens to those that don't?"

"Ah. Well, well, now, there are those, to be sure. They just sort of waste away. Hmmmmm, hmmmm, yes, that's what happens to them. They just waste away." The Teacher shot a sidelong glance up at Seeker. "Though if you want my opinion, I think it's Labyrinth that kills them. Ah, yes, indeed I do! The planet finds a way into their minds, a way to stay there. And then it kills them slowly, but just as surely as if they walked its surface. Aye, it eats them from inside, so to speak. Seeker, the danger here isn't only physical. Labyrinth is deadly to your mind and spirit as well!"

They walked in silence for a few moments. Then Longarm muttered beneath its breath, "Don't know why you do it, I don't. Not by the Primordial Tree I don't." The creature cocked its head to one side and gazed at Seeker with a single eye. "Why, now, do you come here, eh?"

Seeker shrugged. "To become a Questioner, why else?"

"But why become a Questioner at all, eh? Why? Makes no sense. Not a bit. Not even a proper job. You, now, what do you *really* know about Questioners, eh?"

The ursoid gazed moodily off at the distant mountains. "What do I *really* know? No more than most creatures do, I guess. Ummm. Questioners are semi-officials of the Federation. Their job is to wander around the galaxy at random and answer any calls for help that are put out by any planet whatsoever. They jump from star to star until they get a call, then they put their ship in orbit around the planet and project down into the mind of a host."

"Hmmmm, hmmmmm," Longarm mumbled, "standard knowledge, that. And what have you heard about what happens once the Questioner is down on the planet, eh?"

"Well," Seeker began, seeming hesitant, almost apprehensive, "nothing very specific. Just that the Questioner goes around asking questions, looking for a way to solve whatever problem it has been called about. When it finds the answer, it makes its recommendations." Seeker paused, a strange expression crossing its features.

"And then?" Longarm asked.

"And then returns to its ship and jumps to the next system."

Longarm snuffled with humor. "Ah, ah, now that's a pretty piece of fiction! So simple you make it seem! Just ask a few questions and solve the problem! Then zip back up to the ship again and it's off you go!" The Teacher looked up at Seeker, lips curled back from strong yellow teeth in a gesture of derision. "And who says the creatures on the planet have to accept the answer? Or like it even, eñ? Who says they can't hate the solution and just kill the Questioner?"

Seeker looked away, a strange light glowing in its eyes. From behind them Darkhider hissed in shock and confusion. "Kill a Quessstioner? But . . . but sssurely no sssapient creature would kill . . ."

Suddenly serious, the Teacher stopped and turned to look at the group that followed it. "Do you know the kill rate for Novices on their first mission, eh? Thought not. About sixty percent. And for Questioners in general it's about forty percent. That's right. No need to gawk like that."

Addressing them as a group, Longarm continued. "Being a Questioner's a dangerous job, it is. Sure, they're semi-officials of the Federation. But the stress is on the 'semi' rather than the 'official.' And even if they were full officials, what good would it do them, eh? The Federation is a weak thing on purpose. The Empire proved there was no way to police the galaxy. Takes too long, costs too much. Why, the Federation doesn't even have a standing army. And the tiny police force it keeps does nothing but guard some of the major star routes to keep pirates under control.

"What that means is that a Questioner has no authority to enforce its solution to a planet's problem. It has to rely on moral suasion alone. If it can't convince its hosts that its answer is the right one, they can just ignore it. And if its solution angers them . . . well, sapient creatures everywhere in the galaxy have a bad habit of killing those they disagree with. No, the danger doesn't stop when the Novice leaves Labyrinth. It doesn't even stop when the Novice becomes a full Questioner, or even after a hundred missions. Huh, if any have ever lived that long. No, there's no end to it. So even if any of you survive Labyrinth, which is highly doubtful, and even if you make it to full status as a Questioner, which is equally doubtful, there's no end to the death. No end."

Longarm turned back to the path and began to shamble along toward Start once more. As it went, it mumbled to itself. Seeker strode silently by its side. Eventually the Teacher snuck a sideways look at the tall, massive ursoid. "So. Changed your mind, eh?"

"No," Seeker rumbled softly in its wide chest. "No change. I am here. I will try to cross Labyrinth to get to Sanctuary. Maybe I will make it. Perhaps I will die. But I would have died eventually if I had stayed home, so I might as well come here, where I am trying to do something worthwhile, as stay at home where . . . ah, where it didn't matter any more."

"Ah." Longarm nodded sagely. "I see. You come from one of the Solution Planets, eh?"

Seeker stopped in midstride, its eyes wide with surprise. "How . . . how did you know?"

The Teacher pouted out its lips in a smirk. "Solution Planets have all kinds of legends about the glory of Questioners. Damn near make demi-gods of them. Questioners become one of the major role models for the discontented. And there are always plenty of discontented on any Solution Planet!"

Seeker gave Longarm a strange sidelong glance. The ursoid seemed almost uncomfortable talking about the issue. "We almost destroyed ourselves. The Questioner answered our call for help and came to our rescue. If it hadn't been for the Questioner . . ."

"Of course, of course," Longarm interrupted, nodding its shaggy head, "you'd have destroyed yourselves. And you would have, too. Lots of ruins, planetwide ruins, in the galaxy, Seeker. You'd have been just one more. And it wouldn't have made a bit of difference, either. Don't forget that! A Questioner

saved you because you had enough sense to accept the
Solution. But it doesn't make a bit of difference!"

Thisunit spoke up from behind them in protest. "But
sentience is sacred! That's the basic premise behind the
Federation! It's the Prime Directive of the Code! It's . . ."

"It's utter hogwash!" Longarm exploded with a bray of
laughter. "Sentience is as sacred as rotten blurbfruit!
Hmmmm, hmmmm, maybe less sacred, since you can still eat
blurbfruit even when it's rotten. But this is no time to argue
something as stupid as that." The Teacher stopped and gestured with one arm. "We're there. Welcome to Start."

Seeker looked up in surprise. They were standing at the
bottom of a group of buildings that straggled up the hillside.
The buildings were little better than shacks, some made from
weathered and warped wood, others from rusted metal sheets,
and still others cobbled together from what looked like leftover
bits and pieces of packing crates.

Longarm laughed out loud at the look of disgust and
astonishment that flashed across Seeker's face. "Yes, welcome
to Start! What's the matter, Pretender? Not as glorious as you
had envisioned?" The Teacher turned to the others and grinned
at them. "Well, what do you think?"

Bilrog's face showed dismay and anger. "Slaves live in
better quarters on Furmoria," the warrior rumbled.

Longarm shrugged. "I don't doubt it at all. But, then, the
key word is 'live.' You see, you aren't expected to 'live' here
very long. In fact, you aren't expected to 'live' very long at
all!" The Teacher puckered out its lips and gave a loud hoot of
hilarity. "Ah, ah, yes, yes. Make yourselves at home. Wander
around, find a place that suits your individual taste. If you
don't see what you want, just make it yourself. Dig a hole, tear
walls off something else, build a lean-to, whatever. Labyrinth
has almost no axial tilt, so there aren't any real seasons. We're
in a mild zone. Just about this temperature all year round. All
you really need is something to keep the rain off. And maybe
walls for privacy, if that's something your species values, that
is."

The Teacher canted its head to one side and gave them all an
appraising stare. "Sleep well tonight," it said, gentle mockery
in its voice. "It may be the last time you do. Then tomorrow
morning, when the sun rises, you will all gather over there."

Longarm raised a long arm and pointed toward a tall, narrow building that appeared to be made of scrap metal. "That's where most of the Teachers live and where we do our teaching. It's also where we feed you twice a day when you're in Start. Tomorrow you'll be assigned a Teacher and begin your preliminary orientation as Pretenders. Then once you know the basics, someone will take you out on a quick trial run so you get the feel of it. After that," Longarm said, grinning widely, "you'll be pretty much on your own. Any questions? Good. See you all tomorrow."

With those final words and another hoot of amusement, Longarm shambled off in the direction it had indicated.

III.

The five of them stood for several moments and stared silently at the tumble of buildings. Seeker finally shrugged and sighed. "Well, I guess we'll just have to make the best of it."

"This unit cannot extrapolate any other viable alternatives," said Thisunit. "The most logical course of action would be to secure adequate dwelling quarters, and then . . ."

Bilrog growled at Thisunit, flexing razor-sharp claws. "Cease this endless chatter about logic!" The Furmorian turned to face the others. "I will find and occupy the best quarters in Start, regardless of who is in them now. None dare question or resist my power! However, those of you who wish to become my followers may join me, provided you will follow my orders exactly. As a combined force, we will be even more capable of beating Labyrinth."

Darkhider shifted on its feet and darted apprehensive glances in all directions. "It isss getting darker. I can sssenssse the menassse of thisss plassse. Darkhider will leave you all to argue among yourssselvesss. Darkhider goesss to find a sssafe, tight hole to burrow into." Before anyone could respond, the saurian had scampered off into the deepening dusk.

Bilrog looked around at the others. Seeker was murmuring with H*mb*l, and Thisunit was silently contemplating the shacks. Annoyed, Bilrog snorted and turned away. "Very well," the Furmorian warrior said as it stumped off between the shacks, "be on your own! I have no need of such undisciplined companions!"

As Bilrog disappeared, Thisunit moved softly off in a different direction. It offered no goodbyes and received none from the two left behind.

"Well," Seeker commented, "that leaves the two of us. Shall we look together, or do you wish to be alone?"

"I am not used to being alone," H*mb*l replied, "and would be grateful for your companionship, at least here in Start."

"Fine. And perhaps you could tell me more of this idea of dancing Labyrinth. Any particular kind of shack interest you?" the ursoid asked as they began to walk slowly up the hill.

H*mb*l waved its hands in a sign of indifference. "I have preferences, of course, but from the looks of things, they are highly unlikely to be met here in Start. Anything with a roof and walls will do."

"Well, if you don't mind the walk, I'd like to be up high. Someplace where I can look out over the land. I have spent most of my life on a vast plain and feel most comfortable with wide vistas around me and plenty of sky over my head." H*mb*l buzzed agreement, and they began to climb up through the cluster of buildings.

At the very top, they discovered a rather large shack made of ancient, warped boards, odd stones, packing crates, with a roof, open to the sky in two places, made of rusted metal sheets. A rough piece of cloth had been fastened over an opening to serve as a door. They pushed it aside and entered.

"Cozy," Seeker muttered sarcastically, looking around the interior in the last of the evening light. There was only one large, rectangular room, devoid of furniture of any kind. The floor was made of hard-packed earth. "Doesn't seem to have been anyone here for a long time," Seeker snorted as it dumped the sack it had been carrying on the ground in the center of the shack. "Suits me if it suits you."

H*mb*l looked up through one of the holes in the roof. Stars could be seen shining in the sky. "This planet has no satellite, but since it is so much closer to the Center, the night is quite bright with starlight." H*mb*l paused and hummed softly for a few moments. "Yes, this spot will do well. Yes, the sound is right, it feels well." H*mb*l dropped the strange podlike container it had brought off the ship. It knelt beside it and touched it in several places. The pod opened with a sigh and H*mb*l began to take odds and ends from it.

Seeker was taking things from its own sack and placing them on the ground in a corner. "No furniture to put things on or in," it rumbled. "Ah, well, I never had any on the plain. Not ever. Even Nurturers live in the open. In the city beneath Home, yes, there is furniture. But I never really got used to it. I . . ." The ursoid's voice trailed off into a soft mutter as it began to arrange the few things it had brought. Finally, it finished, sat back, placed a small, oblong cake in its mouth and began to chew. "Dinner," it said around the cake, explaining to H*mb*l, who was sitting silently and watching.

When Seeker had finished eating the cake, it licked its fingers and gave a sigh of pleasure. "Those cakes are for journeying. High-energy, compact, light. And very tasty." Seeker bared its teeth in a grimace of pleasure.

"Now," it said as it leaned back against a wall, "tell me more about this dancing. You seemed very upset by what Bilrog and Darkhider said today."

H*mb*l buzzed softly and nodded. "Yes. They do not understand. We are not here to fight and beat Labyrinth. We are here to . . . to . . ."

"To become Questioners." Seeker completed the sentence.

"Yes . . . and no. I mean, we will become Questioners if we manage to cross Labyrinth and reach Sanctuary. But that is not the important thing, that is not the real reason to be here."

Seeker stared at H*mb*l in surprise. "Not the important thing? By all my eggs, H*mb*l, that's the *only* thing! I mean, we're risking our lives here! If it isn't to become a Questioner, what is it for?"

"It's . . . it's . . . so we can dance. I . . . I . . ." H*mb*l stopped speaking and buzzed loudly for a few moments, shifting quickly from foot to foot in evident agitation. "Perhaps the only way I can explain is to tell you the tale of my species."

"Ah," Seeker said with a soft growl of pleasure, "yes, that would interest me a great deal. Yes, tell me."

H*mb*l paused for several minutes, buzzing softly, almost sadly, to itself, preparing its story. Finally it began. "Long and long ago, my people, call us the Hive, lived in great profusion on our planet. We were an industrious and serious race. Our cities spread across the planet, covering every available bit of land. There were billions of us.

"But though we were many, none were hungry, none went without shelter. All belonged, all were part of the Hive. It was a good time, a full time. We were contacted by the Federation and began to go out into the galaxy as traders and workers. Yes, our race was doing well.

"Then it happened. At first it was a small thing, unimportant in the face of larger issues. Here and there a few fell sick. Black spots began to grow on their bodies. The spots spread and became soft and oozed foul juices. There was great pain, the spots became open sores, delirium set in and the sick one died in agony. The mortality rate was one hundred percent, but only a few were affected. There seemed to be no need for panic. Our scientists began to work on it immediately. We even got help from some of the Federation's scientists. We all felt it was only a matter of time until the strange malady was understood and a cure was found for it."

H*mb*l paused and buzzed with distress for several moments. Then it continued. "We were wrong. No cure was found. And the disease began to spread, slowly at first, then more rapidly. Whole areas were sealed off in an attempt to contain the plague, for that was what it had become. Commerce and transportation came to a standstill as whole continents were quarantined. The planet was interdicted by the Federation. No one was allowed on or off the planet. We were on our own.

"In the beginning, most of us didn't know what to do. We just went on living our lives as best we could. Then hivemates, even our egglings, began to fall ill and die around us. Panic set in. There were riots. Quarantined areas broke out in frightened explosions, as those still healthy tried to escape.

"But there was no place left to escape to. Death was everywhere. Every one of us rose each morning and checked our bodies closely, looking for spots.

"When spots were found, many could not stand to live through the pain and horror. They would . . . they would kill themselves. Suicide became an epidemic, second only to the plague itself in its virulence.

"Naturally, our scientists kept trying to find an antidote, a serum, anything that would work, even just slow down the spread of the disease. Many of us kept our faith in them, believing they would succeed.

"Others turned to new leaders who arose from nowhere, promising miraculous cures, offering hopes of all kinds. The plague is a test of our faith in ourselves, some of them said, a test to try our race and make us greater by putting us through the fire. It is taking off only the unworthy, those who have no faith or whose faith is false. So those who felt worthy found hope and joined together to fortify their hope. They staged mass rallies to proclaim their faith and thus prove their worth.

"A different group claimed that the plague was not a matter of the worthy versus the unworthy. Instead, it was a judgement we must bear without protesting. For, they said, we are all unworthy. We can only bow our heads in acceptance. There is nothing to be done, no plan or action that will save us. Struggle is useless. We can only yield to the plague, they counseled. When we have accepted it, it will pass over us and be gone.

"There was one group, however, that could not accept either the idea of giving up or the promise of vain hope. They had a very different view of the plague.

"We have been a proud and successful race, they said. Too proud, too successful. In our self-satisfaction, we have forgotten our origins and our place in the world. We must think long and hard about what we have been and what we have become. So they thought long and hard. And they had many ideas.

"In the beginning, they said, and for many eons after, we lived in harmony with our world. We moved with its rhythms, felt its existence pulsing through our minds and bodies. We were part of the world, and that was as it should be.

"All things in the world have their place and their purpose. It is built right into them, is part of what makes them unique beings. That purpose is theirs and theirs alone. No other thing can share it. For example, the purpose of the poppet is to become a baleroust tree. Nothing else can ever become a baleroust tree and a poppet can never become anything but a baleroust tree. Things might not know their purpose, but they live and die by it all the same.

"And what, they asked, is the purpose of the Hive? The thing that makes the members of the Hive special and unique in nature is that we can know, we are sapient. And since it is evident that nature is knowable, our purpose is clearly to know the world. We are the personification of the knowability of the world. We are the creatures capable of knowing.

"Does knowing itself have a purpose? they wondered. Clearly, particular kinds of knowing have purposes. Knowing how to care for egglings has their health as its purpose. Knowing which tree is a slkaa tree has a purpose when you gather the flowers as food. And knowing a brithworm from a driss has the purpose of avoiding the deadly sting of the driss.

All these particular kinds of knowing have a particular thing or group of things as their object. But what is the object of knowing itself? It can only be the world itself. It can only be the knowing of the purpose of the Hive and how it fits into the purpose of the world. Knowing itself is to let us blend ourselves with the world, to become one with it.

"Yet that was not the way we had used our ability to know. We had conquered nature, plundered it, twisted it to our own ends. We had turned aside from our purpose and taken the wrong path.

"And where had that path led us? We had become the dominant species on the planet. Many other species had perished to make room for our teeming billions, to feed us, to clothe us, to give us living room and places to dwell. But was it right for us to use others for our own ends? Did we have a greater right to live than the flutterers? Than the rummtree? Did we have the right to change the course of a river, to create a lake or destroy one? Just because we were sapient, and therefore the highest achievement of a knowing world, did that give us the right to destroy those things below us in the order? Does it make sense to rip up the foundations of the building to adorn the top?

"The plague was our world's answer to that question. As we had brought other things low, so now some little thing like a virus would bring us low. The plague was a judgement of sorts. But not one against individuals, worthy or unworthy. Instead it was against our whole race.

"What was to be done? Hope was useless; there was none. Almost the entire Hive had been exposed to the plague. Even if a cure could be found, it could not be administered to most of us in time. And no amount of worthiness or faith would stave off the death that awaited those on whom the spots appeared.

"Suicide was equally useless. It was cowardly and resolved nothing. It was simply death in a different form. It was simply doing the plague's work for it.

"But what, then, is left? Only to endure. To walk that fine line between despair and hope. To face the death that surrounded us and to try somehow to *know* it. We must open our minds and our hearts and our ears and try to know and see and hear and feel the world once more. We must try to find our way back to those rhythms to which we once moved in harmony with nature.

"Listen! they cried. Hear the music of the world once more! Do not lock yourselves away in your parts of the Hive, hiding from a death that that can find you anywhere. Come out! Come out! Listen! Hear the music of the world once more! And then dance to it! Dance! Teeter on the very brink of disaster with a light, sure step and a dainty twirl. Dance! they commanded. Move in the world once more, care for the stricken, help your egglings and hivemates. Dance, do, live but do not hope to live. Dance to doom, dance to death, dance to oblivion, dance to life. Move with the plague, move with the surety that soon you will move no more!"

There was a pause in the narrative, filled only with the sound of a slight breeze that blew outside and the even softer humming of H*mb*l. When the creature spoke again, its voice was full of pain and anguish. "Ah, ah, you have no idea what it was like! To watch one's hivemates, some you had even been egglings with, sicken and die in agony, hopeless agony! To see tiny egglings writhe in horror and pain they couldn't even understand! Exquisite anguish!" H*mb*l's voice dropped to the merest whisper. "But worse, far worse was the despair every time you checked your own body for signs of the black spots! Every ache, every pain, every slight twinge seemed to be the onset of a painful death. The most painful of all, the death of self. There was no avoiding it, no pretending, no way to hide it from yourself. Despair! Despair! The horror of utter helplessness!"

H*mb*l fell silent once more. It hummed and buzzed softly to itself for a few moments, then began to move slowly around the room, dancing to unheard music, twirling and stepping to rhythms unknown. Seeker sat and watched in utter fascination. The moves were odd, unexpected, graceful and awkward. They spoke without speaking, expressed anguish and joy, hopeless acceptance and defiant resoluteness. The dance moved and disturbed Seeker for reasons the creature could not even explain.

Eventually H*mb*l stopped and stood silent and still for a long while. Then it began to speak again. "Yes. Some of us took heed of what those others said. We listened and lo! the music was there! So we began to move to it, slowly and hesitantly at first, cringing out into the world like creatures that had hidden long in dark caves, weak and stunned by the brightness of the day. We began to move, awkwardly, poorly, but the more we listened, the more we tried, the more sure we became.

"And finally, we danced. Oh, how we danced! We went into the streets and helped those who lay there abandoned. We went into the worst districts and cared for the dying. We found little ways to ease their pain. And for ourselves, our dance eased the horror, the despair.

"But our race kept dying, dying, dying. The corpses piled up, ten, twenty, fifty deep. We carried them to huge pits and dumped them in. Then we went back and carried more. It seemed an endless nightmare. Death, pain, death. And we danced.

"Eventually, though, the number of new cases decreased. A few of those already ill began to survive. They rose, weak and devastated, and danced along with us.

"The time came when the disease burned itself out. It had killed more than ninety percent of our race. Whole cities stood utterly empty of life. One of our minor continents was totally depopulated.

"The survivors danced through the ruins, cleaning up, saving what could be saved, abandoning what could not be salvaged. Here and there, we discovered other survivors. All had learned the dance, all had found the same way through.

"Where had the disease come from? Where had the dance come from? None of us knew. We only knew that somehow the two were deeply connected. Life had become death for us, and the only answer to it had become the dance. There was a link, a profound link, one that had to be understood in some fashion.

We knew that the future of our race depended on it. There were only a few of us left. A new plague would spell our extinction.

"Some of us realized the only answer lay in the dance itself. In dancing we approached the mystery of the dance itself; it drew us behind it, bringing us forward even as it withdrew. No direct path existed. We could only circle and twirl, step and leap, stamping to the music we heard.

"And then came the realization that the dance itself was the mystery! Doing it was knowing it! It was a circle that turned back on itself, a spiral that went ever inward, each turn coming closer to the center, but never quite reaching it. It was the kind of knowing that we had long ago given up in our pursuit for power and our passion for dominance over nature.

"We knew then where the disease had come from. It had come from us, from the world we had created. It was our planet's judgement on us for taking the path we had taken, for abandoning our original way of knowing the world."

H*mb*l fell silent and still. Seeker stared in wonder at this strange being, knowing there was yet more to come. A vague suspicion was growing in the ursoid's mind. It was beginning to understand H*mb*l's earlier statements regarding its reasons for being there on Labyrinth.

"So," H*mb*l began again at last, "the plague passed on by. And we became a race of dancers, balancing on the thin edge between despair and hope, neither despairing nor hoping, but only dancing, dancing with all our hearts and minds and souls. We danced that we might live and lived that we might dance."

The light dawned over Seeker's mind. "You . . . you . . . came to Labyrinth *because* it is so deadly."

H*mb*l buzzed agreement. "This is the ultimate dance. Labyrinth is even more deadly than the plague was on my home planet. There is nothing deadlier in the whole galaxy. Here despair is at its greatest, hope at its lowest ebb. To be here on Labyrinth is to dance the most perfect dance possible, to walk the thinnest edge imaginable.

"I am here, Seeker, only to dance. It matters not at all if I live or die, if I make it to Sanctuary or not. I am here to dance Labyrinth. That is all."

IV.

Morning came, dim and cloudy. The five met in a tight little knot in front of the building Longarm had pointed out. They seemed to be the only ones in Start.

"Good morning," Seeker greeted them. "Did you sleep well?"

Bilrog snarled. "Of course. I had sensors set all around the perimeter of my shack. The accommodations are primitive, but I am a soldier and am hardened to field conditions."

"This unit does not waste precious time sleeping. It was collecting data all night long. This unit has sampled the air, water, and soil of Labyrinth and has made complete recordings of all night noises. In addition, this unit has taken readings of barometric pressure, relative humidity, wind direction, speed, and other meterological information which allows it to predict a sixty percent chance of a local storm before noon."

Seeker cocked an eye at the lowering, grey sky and nodded. "Brilliant, Thisunit," the ursoid replied drily. "Clearly a great triumph for logic. Though I would give it a lot better than a sixty percent chance."

"The data collected do not support more than a sixty percent chance," the cowled figure protested.

"Ah, but I have better data," Seeker said smugly, tapping its eyes with one paw. "I used an excellent set of sensors. I looked from the top of the hill where our shack is, and I saw it raining off in the distance. Since the rain lay to the west and the wind is blowing from that direction, it follows that . . . and so forth, eh?" The ursoid turned to Darkhider. "Did you sleep?"

"Yesss, now and then. My ssspeciesss never ssssleepsss for more than a few momentsss at a time. We mussst alwaysss be alert for thingsss, dangerousss, hungry thingsss, that might be sssneaking up on usss."

"Not too likely here in Start," said a familiar voice from behind them. They turned and saw Longarm coming out of the building. "Hmmmm. You all made it through the night, eh? Good, very good. No one decided to try out Labyrinth on his own. Oh, don't look like that, no indeed. You'd be surprised how many do exactly that on the first night. Go out and see what the planet is like. Ha! They find out, they do. We usually find a few pieces or maybe just some goo the next morning.

"So, the first thing is to eat. You'll find bowls of some glop on a shelf in there." The Teacher waved a long arm in the direction of the building. "It's what we serve here in Start. Not very tasty, but quite nourishing. No weird proteins to mess up your metabolisms. You were all measured last night, and the glop has been tailored to meet everyone's needs." Longarm cocked its head and shot a quick glance at H*mb*l. "Though I must say it took some doing in your case. You're a strange beast, you are!"

H*mb*l buzzed and bobbed its head. Then it turned away and went toward the building, Seeker by its side. "Mind you," Longarm called out after the five as they entered the building, "bring your bowls back out here. You can eat here. No sense in wasting any time. Best start your orientation as soon as possible."

"Who's to be our Teacher?" Seeker asked as it re-emerged from the building, bowl in hand.

"As rotten luck would have it," Longarm answered, "I'm the only Teacher in Start right now, so I'm saddled with you cripples! Ah, well, it's better than going out on my own. Now sit down, or whatever you do when you eat, shut up, and listen. I'm only going to say things once, so pay attention, eh?"

Longarm glowered around at them and muttered softly beneath its breath for several moments. Then it lowered itself into a seated position, its legs folded beneath it, and began speaking.

"Labyrinth is a very old planet, perhaps the oldest in the galaxy. It is not native to this solar system. It came here on its own from someplace else long, long before most of our races came down out of the Primordial Tree. We don't know where it came from or why. It just did.

"It's the only sentient planet we know of in the galaxy. There are a few that are semi-sentient, but nothing on the level of Labyrinth. This planet controls its own weather, the amount of sunlight that falls on its surface, its axial tilt, its rotation period, its orbit, to mention only a few things. For our purposes, though, the most interesting fact is that it controls the presence of any other form of life on it. Things it likes, flourish. Things it doesn't, die.

"The thing it doesn't like most is other sentient beings. Who knows? Perhaps it was once inhabited by a race that abused it, and now it tries to get rid of sentience other than its own the same way I try to get rid of fleas when I find them on me.

"Whatever the case, Labyrinth is deadly. As soon as you leave Start, it'll try to kill you." Longarm gave them all a sarcastic grin. "Though I may doubt your sentiency, Labyrinth will not.

"How will it try to kill you? Ah, let me count the ways! It will place poisonous things in your path, plants, animals, all with toxins specially adapted to be particularly deadly to your metabolisms. It will create bogs, quicksand, sudden eruptions of boiling mud, crevices will open, rocks come crashing down. Hunting beasts of unimaginable cunning will stalk you from the sky, the water, on the land, even from under it! More clever even than that, if you live long enough, it will develop germs to infect your system and strike you down, burn you up, empty you out.

"But most subtly of all, it will work against your mind. It will never let you rest, will force despair and fear into your every thought, haunt your every waking and sleeping moment with shapes of horror and death."

"Sounds like fun," Seeker muttered beneath its breath.

Longarm laughed loudly. "It is! Oh, it is! I chortle with delight when some poor Pretender limps back into Start with its arm torn off or its face half gone!"

"But surely if the patterns of the planet are carefully observed and logical analysis applied to determine . . ." Thisunit began.

The Teacher clapped its hands and hooted with hilarity. "Thinking won't help you when you're out there! You don't have time to collect data and analyze patterns! You must act and choose." Longarm grabbed a small stone that lay on the ground and suddenly threw it at Thisunit. It struck the cowled figure just below the white mask. "There! You failed to act!"

"This unit tracked the missile, its mass and its velocity and decided it represented no threat. There was no need for evasive or intercept action. Such action would have merely wasted energy."

Longarm gaped at the cowled figure. "This unit's 'thinking time' is measured in nanoseconds, Teacher," Thisunit said,

sounding almost smug. "Full analysis of patterns and projec-
tions of trends takes longer. But do not be deceived that this
unit cannot act just because it thinks. Thinking always precedes
acting, but only by a very short time period."

The Teacher mumbled to itself for a moment, then rose to a
standing position, leaning slightly forward and resting on its
knuckles. "Well, are there any questions? Not that any of you
know enough to ask any. If you're finished with your meal,
then the only thing to do is take the lot of you out for a quick
run. I won't take you anyplace very dangerous. Things around
Start are pretty tame. The further away you get, the worse it
becomes. Huh. I figure Labyrinth is just luring you in deeper
and deeper.

"In any case, stay together. Since you're all different, being
in a group will confuse the planet for a bit, and it won't throw
anything too bad at you too soon. Take it a while to figure out
what to do to whom. But not too long, no sir, not too long at
all. I can promise you that before the day is over at least one
of you will have wounds to show for the experience!"

Longarm glared around at them. "So, then, are there any of
you who want to drop out of this nonsense now while you still
have a chance, eh? Anyone of you smart enough to give it up
before you lose an arm or a leg?" The Teacher's eyes settled on
H*mb*l. "What about you, buzzer?"

H*mb*l hummed a lilting laugh. "I come to dance! There is
nothing to fear. Why would I want to quit?"

Longarm snorted with disgust. "How about you, lizard?"

Darkhider bobbed its head up and down and hissed softly.
"Darkhider knowsss well the danger. Darkhider will ssstay."

"Fool," the Teacher muttered. "And you, Bilrog? Surely a
soldier knows when to cut and run."

"The Furmorians of the Emperor's Guard never ran. Nor
will I. I am here to conquer and conquer I will, or die in the
attempt," the warrior said proudly.

"Most likely, most likely," Longarm said sarcastically.
"Thisunit, you seem a logical sort. No doubt you've figured
the odds quite closely. I'll bet you're staying out of this
foolishness, eh?"

"It is correct to surmise I have calculated the odds for this
unit's survival. It is incorrect to surmise that those odds are not

sufficiently favorable to allow a logical creature to remain in the enterprise. This unit will stay."

Shaking its head in disgust, Longarm finally turned to face Seeker: "And you, my golden friend? Are you as much a fool as the others?"

Seeker grinned broadly. "I must be. I am as ready to face Labyrinth as they are."

Longarm whooped with raucous laughter. "Idiots! Fools! Ah, well, then, if you're all so determined I guess there's nothing for it but to go. Enough of this talking! None of you are worth saving! Enough talking! Time to be doing!" With that, the Teacher swung around and shambled off, motioning them to follow.

V.

They walked single file around the base of the hill occupied by Start to a point where several paths led off in different directions. Longarm stopped and stared at them for some time, as if musing.

"What's the problem?" Seeker finally asked.

"Patience, patience," Longarm mumbled. "I'm trying to remember which was the path the last group of Pretenders took when they left Start."

"Why?" Darkhider queried. "What differenssse doesss it make?"

Longarm turned and leered at the saurian. "Not much, except that they all died because Labyrinth was so lethal along that path. But since this group is in such a hurry to become part of the ninety-three percent, I'll just pick any old path!" With that, the Teacher turned to the furthest left path and set out along it.

Directly behind Longarm was H*mb*l. Next came Seeker, followed by Darkhider and Thisunit. Bilrog brought up the rear with a swaggering step.

They walked for perhaps a half-mile until they came to a small stream lined with short, stunted trees. Longarm pointed to the stream and in a bored voice said, "This is a perfect example of what Labyrinth is like. Last time I was out, there wasn't any stream here. Now there is. Which means the damn

planet has something up its sleeve. We'll go to the left and see
if we can get around it over that way."

Bilrog surveyed the stream with interest. "I see no danger.
The water is fairly shallow and not swift. If necessary, I could
even jump across."

Thisunit approached the stream and bent over slightly to
gaze more closely at it. Then it extended one long sleeve
toward the water. A narrow tube came out, touched the
surface, and then withdrew. The cowled figure rejoined the
others. "This unit would advise against touching the water of
that stream. A quick analysis of it indicates it would be very
poisonous. To be in contact long enough to wade across would
probably be sufficient for the poison to be a lethal dose."

"It isss not only the water," Darkhider hissed softly. "Look
beneath the sssurfasse if your eyesss can. There isss a thing
there, with many armsss and a mouth with many teeth."

H*mb*l buzzed thoughtfully. "There is more. The leaves of
the trees bear a contact poison, and there are tiny creatures on
them that can sting and sting. We must dance carefully here.
We are near the edge. The longer we stay, the more menace
gathers around us. We should move or cross."

"Move," Seeker said, turning to glance at Longarm. The
Teacher nodded and set off once more. The others fell in line.

"There isss sssomething following usss," Darkhider hissed
quietly, pitching its voice just loud enough to reach them all.
Hearing the warning, Bilrog spun around just as a beast about
the size of a wolf launched itself from behind a bush. The thing
had six legs, was covered in shaggy black fur, and had a round
head filled with fangs and eyes. The Furmorian dodged to one
side as the creature leapt at its throat. Bilrog grabbed with
blinding speed and grasped two of the legs on one side. The
warrior spun around itself as an axis and slammed the beast
into the ground with terrific force. The thing screamed in
agony as it smashed into the pebbly soil and then lay still.

"It has ceased functioning," Thisunit declared.

"Damn right it has," snarled Bilrog. "Slow, stupid and
weak. If that's the worst this planet has to offer, this trip is
going to be boring!"

Longarm chuckled. "That's hardly the worst. I told you
before, Labyrinth is just warming up to you. Give it a while.
Your stay, while it may be short, will be anything but boring!"

The Teacher turned and began to lead the way again. In a line, but far more wary now, they walked toward two hills that rose in the distance. "Stream seems to come from there," the Teacher commented. "We can probably get around it on the other side of the hills."

"How do you know where to go?" Seeker asked.

"Don't need to," Longarm grunted. "Not going anywhere."

"But when we go out," the ursoid continued, "we'll be heading for Sanctuary. How do we know which way to go to get there?"

Longarm laughed harshly. "There isn't any way to get there. You just go until you reach it."

"But it has to be in some direction," Seeker protested.

"Why?" Longarm demanded. "Look, Seeker, forget all the rules you learned. Sanctuary isn't anywhere. It's everywhere and it's nowhere. You can get there from here or there or anywhere. But you can't get there by going there."

"Then how are we supposed to find it?"

"You aren't. It finds you."

"That doesn't make any sense," Seeker complained.

"Nothing on Labyrinth does," came the reply, heavy with sneering sarcasm.

There was a sudden squeal of fear and they all stopped dead in their tracks. Darkhider shot off to one side with a speed that dazzled them all. Right on the saurian's trail was a long, slinky creature with many legs that had erupted from the ground in front of Darkhider. Darkhider dodged to the right as the beast leapt forward in an attempt to seize it. Then the saurian doubled back, twisting along its own length in an amazing show of flexibility. The creature overshot its prey and as it went by, Darkhider held out one of the metal implements it had attached to its belt. There was a flash and the smell of burning flesh. The beast shrieked and fell to the ground, biting at its side. It spasmed several times; then, with a soft wail, it died.

Darkhider slunk back into line. "Sssorry. I could have burned it right away, but I didn't want to take a chanssse on burning any of you. It wasss not a very clever beassst, but it wasss dangerousss all the sssame."

"Ah," Bilrog thundered with evident satisfaction, "so the slinker has teeth after all! Those things you carry on your harness are weapons, eh?"

"Weaponsss?" Darkhider replied. "No, they are . . . protectionsss, amuletsss, thingsss given by the Godsss of the Ssslime."

"But that was a burner, wasn't it?" Bilrog asked, his face showing his confusion over Darkhider's denial.

"Yesss, thisss time it burned, for that wasss appropriate. But nexssst time it might cut. It isss not a weapon. It isss a . . . a *power* given me by the Godsss. I . . . sssometimesss it may be usssed to heal inssstead of dessstroy. I'm sssorry. There isss no way to exsssplain . . ."

They all moved off in silence, all senses on the alert now, scanning the sky, the landscape, even the ground they walked on. Danger, they had finally fully realized, could come from anywhere.

Longarm stopped suddenly and snorted. "Huh! What's this?" The Teacher stood and stared ahead, gazing intently at the ground. "Odd," it muttered. "Odd indeed."

H*mb*l stepped next to Longarm. "I see it, too. Many small pits, each with a hair in its middle." Longarm nodded thoughtfully. "But there is more," H*mb*l continued dreamily. "There is a strange sound in the air, a vibration. Ah, ah, it is coming from the hairs! They are all vibrating slightly, do you see?"

The Teacher sighed. "Yes, now I do. I fear we had best turn back and try to find another way."

"Why?" Bilrog demanded. "Surely you're not afraid of that!" the warrior snarled with contempt, gesturing at the flat ground in front of them.

"Oh, yes, very much so," Longarm replied seriously. "And you would be, too, if you knew what it was. Allow me to enlighten you." The Teacher sighed. "I have only seen it once before and I will never forget that time. It was slightly different that time, but enough alike to alert me.

"Oh, yes, I remember well." Longarm paused, its forehead creased with a deep frown, its smiling lips drawn down suddenly in a grimace. "It was many years ago when I was first on Labyrinth and I was still naive. That whole area out there is one being. Those hairs that stick up are its sensing devices. They vibrate at a certain frequency. If anything comes between one hair and another, the vibrations are thrown off. The progress of a creature can be followed very exactly across the area by simply following the disturbance of the vibrations of the hairs. When the prey is in the center, the creature, which is lying spread out under the whole area, folds up out of the ground and wraps around its prey. Its a thin thing and you might be able to cut your way out, if you had a sword ready." Longarm gestured toward the area covered with the pits and the hairs. "It's bigger now than it was then. It could catch all of us. I . . . I've seen what it can do. I . . . there's nothing to do but back up and find another way." They were all shocked to see how disturbed and worried Longarm was. It made every one of them feel a sudden chill of fear.

The Teacher began to turn away. H*mb*l held out a hand and detained it. "Wait, Longarm. This creature depends on its vibrations. If they are thrown off, if they are confused, what would it do?"

"I don't know," Longarm admitted. "I can't imagine how you could even do such a thing. The minute you walk out there between those hairs . . ."

"But if you don't walk . . ." H*mb*l hinted with a wry buzz. "If instead you dance in time with it, hum its own tune." H*mb*l turned to face them all. "Watch me, wait until I call or return here for you. Then follow in my steps as closely as you can. We will cross."

H*mb*l began to move out across the area, humming loudly and moving with a swaying, dancing motion. The creature's feet barely seemed to touch the ground. They watched with wonder as H*mb*l began to twirl and sweep, to bob and spin here and there among the hairs. Soon they could all see the hairs waving this way and that, some rapidly, some slowly. The ground began to heave rhythmically, rippling as the hairs did, keeping time to a rhythm they could all feel but not understand.

H*mb*l circled around the area twice, then moved closer and closer to where they still waited. When the creature was once more right in front of Longarm it said, "Now. Follow. Dance with me and my partner. Move to the music I will sing for you. If you can, sing along." H*mb*l began to buzz and hum more loudly, its tones rising and falling as if they were indeed a strange song, a liturgy sung by a million bees. Behind, the others moved in a line, following the steps of the creature as best they could, each in its own way, according to the form and limits of its own body. And one by one, they began to sing along with H*mb*l.

Before any of them realized it, they were on the far side of the menace. They looked back in awe, watching the tiny hairs waving and vibrating, and the ground rippling and heaving, still keeping time with the dance and the song. The sound of it died in their throats as they understood they were safe. H*mb*l was still standing at the edge of the area, swaying and humming. Then slowly, it fell silent, and the hairs stopped swaying and became calm once more.

H*mb*l stood quietly before them, wrapped in thought. Finally it buzzed softly and said, "You see, there was no need to destroy, no need to smash into the ground, no need to burn."

"That thing could have killed you," Seeker declared flatly.

"Oh, yes, certainly. In fact, it was quite close to doing so on several occasions." H*mb*l sounded excited and pleased. "Yes, very close. But that was still no reason to kill it. The real problem wasn't how to destroy it, but rather how to seek and find a . . . a balance with it."

"To make it into a dance partner," Seeker muttered.

"Yes! Precisely," H*mb*l replied.

Longarm shook its head. "Well, whatever. It worked . . . this time. But I know that creature, and H*mb*l is right, it was near to killing him more than once." The Teacher gave H*mb*l a long look. "If you want my advice, I'd not go near it again for a long time, not until it's had a chance to forget what you did." Longarm turned from H*mb*l and swept its eyes over the rest of the group. "Best not to stand around too long in one place on Labyrinth. Damn planet starts sending things to you, and it can get pretty thick if you don't keep moving. So, let's go."

The Teacher led them around the rightmost of the two hills. The ground in this area, and especially between the two hills, was littered with boulders, some no bigger than a head, others nearly twice the size of Bilrog. Since they offered excellent lurking space for enemies, everyone walked with even greater caution than usual.

Longarm pointed off to the left into the valley between the hills. "Ah, there. As I thought. The stream starts there." They could see a spot about two hundred yards off where water was bubbling up out of the ground and then flowing off to form the stream they had been trying to get around.

Bilrog growled and said, "Wait here. I have a score to settle." Without waiting for a reply, the Furmorian strode off through the boulder field toward the spring. Without asking permission, Thisunit scampered after the warrior. The rest, responding to a gesture from Longarm, stayed put.

Bilrog walked to the side of the spring and stared at it for several moments, as if calculating. Thisunit arrived by his side, dipped his tube in the water and said something to the Furmorian. Bilrog nodded and looked around as if searching for something. Finding what he wanted, he took three steps to a boulder, knelt next to it, wrapped his arms around it, and with a mighty heave, lifted it from the ground. Then he walked back to the spring, slowly lifted the boulder over his head and slammed it down into the spring. It fit perfectly. Quickly then, Bilrog brought other boulders and piled them on top of the first until the spring was obliterated. With a final look at his handiwork, Bilrog brushed his uniform off and, with Thisunit scampering along behind, rejoined the group.

Longarm looked at the two of them and shook its head in disgust. "There is a creature that lives in these boulder fields, generally it burrows under the boulders. It's about three feet long, has eight legs, a large, black, furry body, a head full of very sharp teeth, and only one thing on its mind: eating alive anything it comes across. I've seen Pretenders enter boulder fields like the two of you just did and go down under a swarm of the things. In about two minutes, the only things left of them were the larger bones, provided they had any to begin with. You're fools, both of you."

"This unit did not detect the presence of any living being among the boulders," Thisunit declared. "It is evident from both the surface of the ground and that of the boulders that this field is of recent origin, and therefore the creatures you mentioned have possibly not taken up residence here yet."

The Teacher snorted with disgust. "Don't put too much stock in your damn sensors, Thisunit. Experience is clear on . . ."

"This unit's sensors are very accurate. More so than your own organic ones. And as for 'experience,' this unit prefers to gather current data and use them as the basis for extrapolation as opposed to blindly accepting previous readings as eternally pertinent."

"Are you saying you don't draw generalizations, don't make general assumptions?" Seeker asked in surprise.

"If by assumptions you mean deciding in advance which data are relevant and which are not, the answer is no."

"But how do you avoid being inundated? I mean, how can you sort out the almost infinite amount of input and make any sense of it without assumptions to filter out most of it and pick only the things that matter?"

"All data are valid, all data matter. None must ever be excluded. Each datum is unique and precious. As for a pattern, one will automatically emerge when, and only when, as many factors as possible are accounted for. Even then, before one can be certain of its validity, the pattern must be tested again and again with new data to make sure it is complete."

Seeker looked dismayed. "Thisunit, do you mean to say that you have no collective words in your language? No words that stand for groups of similar things? Do you mean that every datum is seen as unique and treated as such, that each has its own designation, its own word?"

"Precisely." Thisunit gestured with a long sleeve toward the boulder field that surrounded them. "That boulder over there to the right is not the same as the one Bilrog threw in the spring to block it. In Federation Common you have these class words like 'boulder,' and then you add predicate descriptives to differentiate one from the other. This usage makes a totally incorrect presupposition about the relative identicality of the two objects. In this unit's language, each boulder has a discrete denomination and is treated as a totally separate and unique entity. This unit's language is thus very rich in significance. This unit finds Federation Common a weak and impoverished language, poorly suited to analysis."

Longarm chuckled. "Without a doubt, this is the weirdest bunch of Pretenders I've ever had the displeasure of teaching. I know you are fascinated by Thisunit's linguistic explanations, Seeker, but may I suggest we move it? The longer we stand here jawing about how pathetic our dear old Federation Common is as a language for analysis, the longer Labyrinth has to get our range and send something out to analyze us all into a nice meal."

The Teacher turned to Bilrog. "Just one thing, though. What in the name of the Primordial Tree was the point of heaving the boulders in the spring?"

"It was a declaration of war," Bilrog stated solemnly.

Longarm gaped in wonder at the Furmorian, then threw up its arms and gave a hoot of laughter. "Declaring war on a planet! By the Tree, the whole lot of you is daft! Weirdest bunch I've ever seen." Longarm chuckled heartily as it turned and led them off again.

They passed out of the boulder field as they left the area of the two hills and came to a rolling grassland that stretched off until it ran up against a range of hills. Seeker sighed on seeing it. "Almost like Home," the honey-colored creature murmured.

"Aye, but all the more reason to be wary," Longarm advised. "If you think of it as home, you'll be looking for all the things that were dangerous at home. Here they could be wildly different. Take that little yellow flower over there. Don't ever try to cross a big patch of them. They exude an odor that is quite sweet and quite deadly. In large quantities, they produce enough to put you to sleep. You'll never wake up again. Now over there . . ."

"Down!" Seeker roared in a voice so full of command that the other five dropped to the ground without thinking. When they looked up, Seeker was several paces off, running across the plain, with several large, winged creatures flapping about its head. Two more lay lifeless on the ground at the spot where the ursoid had first cried out. Even as they watched, two more fell in tangled, shattered heaps to the grass. A fifth and sixth, with screams of anger and frustration, flapped heavily back up into the sky.

Seeker picked up one of the fallen creatures and brought it back to the other five travelers, who were getting to their feet. The ursoid held the winged creature out to Longarm. It had a wingspan of a good five feet. The body was small and the head large, with a massive beak filled with sharp teeth. Hanging from the body were four clawed legs. "Flyers. Teeth, claws, and very keen eyesight. They were circling way up high. When they got our range they swooped and attacked. I saw them at the last minute. Huh. I must be getting sloppy in my old age. Should have noticed them right off."

Longarm took the flyer from Seeker and stared at it. "Never seen anything quite like that before." The Teacher handed it back to Seeker, who casually threw it aside. "Hmmmmm. Well, I think that's about enough for one day. Yes, indeed I do. You may not realize it, but we've been out for most of the day."

"Sunset is in three hours, seventeen minutes and twenty-one seconds," Thisunit announced.

Longarm looked surprised. "Ummm, yes, of course. So we had best be heading back. You've all survived, and that's not bad for a first day's work. Not at all. There might be some hope for the whole miserable lot of you after all. Some, but not much."

The Teacher paused and canted its head to one side, as if listening to something. "Hmmmmm, hmmmmm, yes. I think we should head back right away. I sense a sort of lull; can any of you feel it? Labyrinth has realized we are here and is considering what to do about it, yes. If we hurry, we just might get back to Start before any decision is made and action taken. Stay with me. I'm going to go pretty fast, so don't lag or stray. Yes, let's take advantage of this lull." With that, the Teacher turned and began to lope off, using arms and legs for enhanced speed. The others fell into line and followed.

Seeker was surprised to find that H*mb*l had dropped back and was keeping pace on the left. "You seem preoccupied with thought," H*mb*l said with a worried buzz. "Is something wrong?"

For a few moments Seeker didn't reply. Then the ursoid sighed deeply and said, "I don't really know if 'wrong' is the right word, H*mb*l. But there is something strange going on, and there's no doubt about that."

H*mb*l buzzed softly with interest. "And what is that?"

"Well," Seeker replied, "perhaps I'm just imagining things, but it seems to me that Longarm knew exactly where it was taking us. Somehow the surprise the Teacher showed at the things we met seemed . . . contrived, acted, false. It was almost as if it knew precisely what was going to happen, when, and where. I would swear that Longarm dropped just an instant before I called out."

They ran along beside each other in silence for several moments. Then Seeker said, "And there's another thing. Did you notice how each one of us was posed a problem? And how in every case, the problem was matched to our own abilities? Bilrog was attacked by a large, fierce animal which required strength and trained warrior skills to defeat. Darkhider needed speed and evasiveness. You had to dance. On two occasions Thisunit had to analyze. And I . . . I met with a creature that is reminiscent of killbirds and other dangerous flyers on my own planet."

"But Longarm said that Labyrinth tailors its deadliness to match our weaknesses."

"Our weaknesses, yes. But this time it matched our strengths. It gave each one of us a problem we were most likely to be able to handle." Seeker was quiet for a moment, then spoke softly, musingly. "And I can't help but wonder how it knew so quickly. Did it find out? Or was it told?"

"Told? But . . . but who could tell it?"

"H*mb*l, do you think it was chance that Longarm was on the ship with us? And chance that Longarm is the only Teacher in Start? And that it was Longarm who has taken us on our first trip onto Labyrinth?

"I wonder, H*mb*l, just how far the power of Labyrinth reaches. Could it send a part of itself off-planet? Could it create its own Teacher?"

They ran in thoughtful silence until the shacks of Start appeared in the distance.

VI.

Dinner consisted of another bowl of gruel, this time of lumpy consistency and slightly sour to the taste. When the meal was completed, Longarm addressed them all, saying, "Well, you made it through your first day on Labyrinth. Hopefully you all now understand how deadly the planet actually is. If you had gone out alone, none of you would have returned alive, and I would have had to eat all this gruel by myself.

"But tomorrow, that's exactly what you will have to do: go out there on your own. Oh, you can go as a group if you want to, but I wouldn't recommend it. Too big a target, especially now after today since Labyrinth will be waiting for the group again. If you go individually, you'll create a new confusion and have a better chance for a day or so.

"Anyway, do what you want to do. You can even stay in Start if you're too frightened to go out. If any of you want to ask me anything, I'll be around." With a final leer at them all, Longarm turned and entered the building reserved for Teachers.

The five Pretenders sat for a few more moments. Then Bilrog rose and declared, "I go out. If you were wise, you would join me in my war against this planet. Accept my command and you will increase your chances of survival."

"Darkhider will go out, too," the saurian said. "But Darkhider will creep about carefully, not ssstump and rage and roar. Darkhider will go ssso quietly that Labyrinth will not even notissse."

All eyes turned to rest on Thisunit. The cowled figure shifted uncomfortably beneath the united stares. "This unit will spend the dark period of this planet's cycle gathering further data. Then when the light period commences, it will go out onto the surface again to continue its data collection and collation. When it has adequate extrapolations, well within the ninety-five percent range, it will proceed to Sanctuary."

H*mb*l hummed softly. "I, too, will go forth in the morning. For I long to continue the dance." Bilrog snorted, but not so derisively as before. H*mb*l's recent performance had impressed them all, including the Furmorian warrior.

Seeker sat looking at the ground. When the ursoid realized it was now the only one that had not stated its intentions, it lifted its eyes to the sky. "Of course I'll go out," it said gently, almost absently, as if its mind was far away. "After all, that's why I'm here." Seeker's eyes came down from the sky to rest on each of the other Pretenders for a moment before moving on to the next. The gaze was focused now, keen and enquiring. "What I'm not sure I understand is why the rest of you have come. H*mb*l I know about because it told me. But you, Bilrog, for instance, I can't imagine why you are here. I don't think you come from one of the Solution Planets. Certainly becoming a Questioner would not be an advancement for one who is a mercenary soldier, since I imagine you could find a much higher, more responsible position within the Federation police force. I know I, for one, would be thankful to have a warrior like you guarding the space lanes against pirates.

"Or you, Thisunit. How could you want to become a Questioner? Aside from the fact that Questioners gather data by asking questions, they reach their answers through inspiration rather than cold analysis. I can't see that appealing to you or your race.

"Darkhider. You're the biggest mystery of all. A race that has survived by avoiding danger sends one of its own into the greatest danger in the galaxy. Not by chance, but on purpose. It makes no sense. It's totally against everything your evolution stands for." Seeker shook its shaggy head. "No, the whole lot of you don't make much sense.

"But there's another thing that bothers me even more. You're all, with the exception of H*mb*l, so *obvious*. In fact, you're almost living symbols. Bilrog is clearly brute strength and force. Thisunit stands for logic. Darkhider is cowardice. It's . . . it's as if someone was trying to . . . to make a point. I . . . I'm not expressing it too clearly, but . . ."

"And you," Darkhider hissed, "what do you ssstand for? You sssay you find usss obviousss. Did it ever occur to you that we might find you the sssame? Did you ssstop to think that to me, for exsssample, the ressst of you ssseem mere ssstereotypesss and I am the deep, complexsss one? You Ssseeker, are a virtual prototype of the Slime God known asss Multi . . . ah, thisss confounded Federation Common lacksss the consssseptsss . . . Multidoingsss isss the bessst I can do. Oh, yesss, I ssseem sssimple to you, but that isss only becaussse you know ssso little about me."

"Darkhider is correct," Thisunit joined in. "Your style of analysis, as you indicated earlier, Seeker, depends on the setting up of universal categories derived from a relatively small number of data. In simple terms, you think by generalizing. This is probably due to the paucity of your sensory devices and the very narrow limits within which they operate. It is clear to this unit that your planet is a very impoverished one with a fairly steady environment that allows for generalizations. This unit would like to point out that . . ."

Seeker laughed and held up its hands. "All right, all right! I yield! You win! I'm judging on the basis of insufficient data! I apologize to all of you."

"Not so fast," Bilrog said. "You were going somewhere with your idea. Where?"

Seeker hesitated as if trying to decide. "Ah, well, it's probably nonsense, but I almost wondered if some of you weren't actually part of Labyrinth itself."

The sounds of dismay and protest were instant and loud. It was Bilrog who cut them off impatiently. "Go on. There's more, isn't there? What do you mean by that?"

"Well, it occurred to me that if the planet is really so intelligent and so determined to destroy us, wouldn't one obvious technique be to plant a spy in our midst to find out as much as possible about us?" The others nodded in agreement, their growing interest encouraging Seeker to continue. "Also, didn't all of you notice how the things that came against us today were all so well matched to our strengths?"

Bilrog muttered a curse. "You're right! That thing that launched itself at me was not far from a skarlhound in size, speed, and tactics. I hunted them barehanded as a youth. Everyone does."

Darkhider blinked with agitation. "The ssslinker that attacked me, yesss! I have ssseen itsss like before! By the Original Egg, it never occurred to me . . ."

"Your point is well made, Seeker," Thisunit stated. "Though the data are few and conclusions based on them are at best shaky, this unit would like to hear the rest of your analysis."

"Well," Seeker continued thoughtfully, "the analysis gets even shakier now, Thisunit. Let's assume that what I have suggested is true, and Labyrinth is capable of sending a spy. What would it send? A complex body, to be sure, a real being selected, perhaps, from those on its surface. But since none of those are sentient, it would also have to make it appear intelligent so it could mingle with the rest of us. Could it create intelligence? Perhaps, though that is a much more difficult task than merely producing a physical entity. The simplest thing would be to create a simple intelligence, one that was one-dimensional, one that was a stereotype."

"One," Bilrog muttered in a thoughtful whisper, "that was simply brave, simply cowardly, simply logical."

"Yes," Seeker nodded. "And that is why I wondered about you and Thisunit and Darkhider. You seem to be that way."

Bilrog laughed. "As you seem to me!"

"As you all appear to this unit," added Thisunit.

They all looked sideways at each other with suspicion. "There might be sssomething to what you sssay," Darkhider murmured, hunching down nervously, its eyes swiveling more furiously than ever. "There isss nothing sssure on Labyrinth. Not even usss."

For several moments they all sat wrapped in private thoughts and in the growing darkness of the approaching night. Finally, Bilrog rose and addressed them all. "I take back my offer of alliance. Tomorrow I go out to make war on Labyrinth, and I will go on my own. There is something strange going on here, and I am not sure I can depend on any of you. I want no fifth column behind my back! Good night." Without another word, and without a backward glance, the Furmorian stumped away.

Slowly, the others parted without more than muttered good nights and passed silently through the pathways of Start in search of their shelters.

Soon Start was as silent as the night itself.

VII.

Longarm watched the five Pretenders eat their breakfast, a sardonic smile curving its full lips. "My, my," the Teacher said finally, "aren't we a solemn lot this morning! Hmmmm. Yes. I imagine we have all suddenly realized we might die today. More than one Pretender has died its first day out, let me tell you! Why, I remember once when the whole lot was killed, hmmmm, yes. Must have been four or five of them. They . . ."

"Is this part of teaching, Longarm?" Seeker asked softly. "This constant harping on the idea of our deaths, this endless chipping away at our self-confidence? Whose side are you on, anyway?"

"Side? Whose side am I on? Ah, Seeker, such a fool! And I thought you were the bright one in this miserable crowd! There are no sides here. There is only life or death. And of that pair, death is by far the stronger.

"You complain that I chip away at your self-confidence. Perhaps you misunderstand, my furry friend. Perhaps your self-confidence is your own worst enemy. Ha!" Longarm rocked back and forth in explosive laughter. "Oh, yes, yes, your own worst enemy indeed! Why do you suppose, Seeker, that each Pretender is only allowed a very limited amount of baggage? Heh? Wonder about that? Well, it's obvious, it is. If we let you bring what you wanted, you Pretenders would bring all kinds of fancy weaponry. Like Bilrog there. I'll bet our warrior would have brought laser beam weapons at the very least. Ha! See, I'm right, the Furmorian's nodding. Instead, there were limitations, and what did Bilrog bring, eh?"

"Two good knives, some rope, a canteen, a lightweight personal shield, duralloy mesh armor for my chest, two changes of clothes, a fire starter, first aid kit, and some field rations. About forty pounds in all," the warrior rumbled.

"Hmmmmm. Good choice except for the personal shield. I'd throw it away if I were you. The point, Seeker, is that the less protection you bring, the fewer gimcracks you drag around with you, the more frightened you'll be and the more alert and careful. Come here with a powerful laser rifle and you won't last half an hour. Too cocky, too confident.

"Yes, I'm trying to frighten you all. Damn Pretenders always start out with too much confidence. Believe all the myths about Questioners. Idealistic crap. They waltz out there onto the surface of Labyrinth and snip, snap, they're dead.

"But those who creep out, fear keeping every sense tuned so finely they sense intention before action begins, ah, ah, they come back!

"Now this lot, all of you, you're all too damn sure of yourselves. Even Darkhider is so sure of its cowardice that it thinks nothing will catch it unaware. Ha!" Longarm's sarcastic tone suddenly became serious. "Mark my words, all of you. Be afraid. Be very, very afraid! I don't know which of you will be the first to die, but I can guarantee it won't be long until one of you does."

The Teacher sat back and looked at them with mild disgust. "I'm going to do something I don't ordinarily do. But you're all such a bunch of dunderheads I have no choice. I'm going out today when you do and keep sort of loose tabs on the lot of you. I'll be off away from you, just checking you out. If you get into some really serious trouble that I can help with, I'll do what I can. But don't count on me. I might not be there when you need me, and I might not be able to do anything even if I am.

"You're on your own, Pretenders. More on your own than ever in your lives. I wish you well." With that, Longarm rose and shuffled back into its quarters.

For several moments they sat silently and looked at each other from the corners of their eyes. Finally Bilrog stood. "I go. I will take the opposite path from the one we took yesterday. Farewell. May we meet this evening."

As the Furmorian strode away, Thisunit sighed and began to move off in the same direction. "This unit will depart as well. This unit will retrace the journey of yesterday and continue its mapping of the planet. This is the only logical procedure. Once the mapping and analysis is properly made, proceeding to Sanctuary will be a simple matter."

Darkhider rose and cast quick looks at H*mb*l and Seeker. "It isss time to go. Longarm isss wrong. I am not confident of my cowardissse. I will go ssslowly and carefully, alwaysss afraid." The saurian, casting nervous glances to all sides, scuttled off toward the edge of Start.

Seeker growled gently and stood, stretching. It adjusted the pouch it wore strapped around its waist, making a mental inventory of its contents one more time: a knife, a short piece of rope, first aid material, a small quantity of food. Ready, Seeker looked over at H*mb*l and said, "Probably be best if we went alone this first day, H*mb*l. We should each get a feel for the planet in our own way."

H*mb*l buzzed gentle agreement. "I can always hear the music best when I am alone, Seeker. I thank you for understanding." With a stiff bow, the creature moved off smoothly, almost as if already making the first steps of its dance.

Seeker followed slowly. When the ursoid finally reached the place at the edge of Start where the paths led off in different directions, there was no sign of any of the others. Seeker turned and looked back at the cluster of shacks. Longarm was nowhere to be seen. Seeker wondered about what the creature had said. It made a certain amount of sense, and yet . . .

With a sigh, Seeker picked a direction and set off. The day was clear and the sun hot. Seeker estimated that this planet was slightly smaller than its own native world and probably closer to its primary. The primary was also bluer than the one that warmed Seeker's world.

A ridge ran parallel to Seeker's route on the left, and the ursoid decided to climb it for a better view of the area. Once at the top, Seeker gazed about with curiosity. Everything seemed so calm and normal. To the left was a marshy area along a small stream that meandered off to the north and south. Even on its home world, Seeker's kind had avoided marshy areas. Best to do so here as well. To the north, the land rose steadily until it formed a range of low, abrupt hills. To the right, east, a plain ran off, dotted here and there with groves of some kind of tree. South lay Start.

Seeker sucked in great lungfuls of air, testing for dangerous scents. Silly, it reminded itself. The things that smelled dangerous at home aren't even here. And those that are dangerous here I don't even know the smells of yet. But everything seems so calm. Even the sky is clear of those flying things that attacked yesterday. Seeker sucked in more air and was suddenly reminded of a time long, so long, ago when it had stood on another ridge and looked off into the distance. A shudder passed through it at the memory, a shudder of pain as well as of delight. So fast then, so swift. It had flown that day. Nearly.

The ursoid shook itself back into the present. Dangerous, Seeker scolded itself. Keep your sense about you. Remember the past some other time. Stay in the present now. It's the dangerous thing. But then, it admitted, so is the past.

Seeker remembered what Longarm had said about standing too long in one place and decided it was time to move. I'll follow this ridge to the north and that range of hills.

The ursoid began to walk slowly along the top of the ridge, keeping a sharp lookout in every direction as it went. There were some boulders and loose rock up ahead and to the left, just at the edge of the ridge. Seeker didn't like the look of it. Perfect place for a creature to hide, it thought. Yet there was no way past it unless the ursoid climbed down the ridge. Well, then, Seeker decided, I go past carefully and . . .

Three furry things shot out from under one of the rocks and launched themselves at Seeker's throat. The ursoid threw itself to one side even as it grabbed one of the creatures by the neck and flung it over the edge of the ridge. Seeker hit the ground and sprang to its feet, spinning around just in time to meet a second attack from the two remaining animals. It was almost pitifully easy. In a moment, they both lay dead at Seeker's feet.

The ursoid stared at them in utter disbelief. They were small, hardly bigger than a rabbit. They had teeth and claws that were a definite menace to another of their species, but hardly anything for a creature of Seeker's size to worry about. On Seeker's home world, such creatures would have avoided attacking and simply let him pass. Why had they struck with such mindless ferocity?

Seeker heard a soft mewling sound coming from the rocks. Cautiously it crept forward, following the sound. There, beneath one of the boulders, was a nest filled with seven tiny copies of the creatures he had just killed. A nest. No wonder they had attacked. They were defending their young against . . .

But this is Labyrinth! It was the planet that was trying to kill him. And yet . . . the attack was totally logical, totally explicable in ordinary terms. One didn't need to posit a hostile, sentient planet to understand what had just happened. One only had to think of . . .

The blow knocked the ursoid sideways into the rock. A second flyer smashed into the rock where Seeker had been just a moment before. Seeker rolled in time to avoid the attack of a third. The ursoid jumped up and grabbed the flyer that had hit the rock. It was dazed and shaking its head. Seeker killed it with one blow to its scrawny neck and then flung it, just in time, at the flyer that was diving for its second attack. The dead creature slammed into the diving one and they tumbled to the ground together. Seeker leapt to its feet and then dodged to one side as the third attacker swooped in. The ursoid struck the flyer on the neck and it fell dead to the ground.

The second creature was still trying to disentangle itself when Seeker stepped up to it and dispatched it with a swift kick to the head. It tried to bite the foot that killed it, but wasn't fast enough. Seeker stepped back, crouched into a defensive position, and scanned the air and ground around it. No more.

Pain hit then. The whole left shoulder was on fire. Seeker reached up and its hand came away sticky with blood. Ah. The first attack, the one that had sent it sprawling against the rock and saved it from the second flyer. Seeker probed the wound with deft fingers and assessed the damage. Nothing too bad. Just a few surface scratches. It rummaged around in its pouch for an ointment it carried there, and soon the pain was gone and the wound already on the mend. Just as good as new in a few days, Seeker told itself, though it will slow me down a bit for the moment.

Should I head back to Start? The decision was instant. No. I haven't been out more than a few hours. To go back now . . . How Longarm would howl with laughter! And the look on Bilrog's face . . . No. I'm almost as good as new. Just have to be a bit more careful, that's all.

Seeker started off north along the ridge again. Finally the ridge narrowed to nothing and the ursoid climbed down and followed the stream, though staying a good distance from the water after yesterday's experience. By midday, Seeker had reached the hills and eaten a quick meal while sitting on the crest of the first of them. The view was good in all directions. Nothing could come within several hundred yards without being seen.

Its meal over, Seeker decided to go a short way into the hills before turning back for Start. Three hills in, standing in the bottom of a sharp, deep gully between two hills, it realized it had made a very bad mistake. Something was stalking it.

Seeker stood very still and listened with all its might. It sniffed the air. There was a strange, pungent smell on the breeze, an odor that reeked of death and blood and . . . There, that shuffling noise again. And that whuffing, snuffling intake of air. Slowly Seeker backed against the steep side of the gully and prepared itself. It reached into its pouch and withdrew the short, sharp knife it kept there. Bilrog isn't the only one with an extra claw, it thought. Ever since I lost my natural ones, I've had a nice little one of metal. Just in case, just in case.

The creature came around the bend in the gully and saw the prey it hunted. Seeker growled at it, studying it. It was somewhat shorter than the ursoid, vaguely feline in looks. It walked on all fours. Its front legs were powerful and longer than its rear ones. It had a massive chest that made its strength even more apparent. Four beady eyes glared at Seeker, judging, estimating. A pink tongue lolled out and the mouth opened to show short but very sharp teeth. It moaned softly and stepped slowly forward.

With a thunderous hiss it launched itself at Seeker. The ursoid waited until the last moment, then threw itself forward and to the left toward the opposite wall of the gully. Its right arm swept out, though, the knife held in the fist so that it stuck out of the top. The blade struck flesh and ripped as Seeker twisted and rolled.

The creature spun, and almost faster than Seeker could turn was in the air for another strike. The ursoid tried to dodge again but was too slow. The beast struck Seeker's right shoulder and sent the ursoid sprawling. It was on its downed opponent in a flash, and the two of them rolled in a desperate battle on the floor of the gully. The creature slashed Seeker several times, trying to grab the throat. Seeker slashed and hacked with its knife, feeling blood flowing freely and knowing it was not all the creature's.

They thrashed and rolled around in a wild melee. Seeker felt itself weakening, but knew it was killing the creature just as surely. *If only I can last a little longer . . .* Seeker got its arm free and brought the knife up, slamming it into the side of the creature's head again and again.

With a moan that came from somewhere deep in its chest, the creature opened its mouth and a gush of hot blood poured out. A gigantic spasm shook the beast and then it slumped, its weight atop Seeker. For several moments the ursoid just lay there, exhausted, trembling, unsure if it was dying itself. Then it realized that the smell of the blood and the noise of the struggle were bound to draw other predators. Weakly, Seeker struggled out from under its opponent and began to crawl away.

The ursoid crawled down the gully until it had put two bends between itself and the dead beast. Then slowly, carefully, it began to take stock of its situation. Its left shoulder was badly mauled, the bones probably broken and the flesh grimly lacerated. Blood was flowing freely from many wounds. The right leg was badly damaged where the beast's claws had raked it again and again. The right side of the face was ripped open and the right ear was a tattered, shredded mess.

Seeker growled deep in its chest. *Other than that, I'm in great shape.* Methodically, it set to work applying what first aid it could give itself with the supplies it carried in its pouch. Next time I won't leave the pain killer at home, it told itself grimly as it winced from the throbbing pain that almost drove it unconscious. If there is a next time.

Finished, Seeker looked up at the sky and tried to estimate the time. Late. Much too late for a wounded Pretender to make it all the way back to Start on its own before nightfall. It shuddered. Night on Labyrinth was said to be even more deadly than day. Seeker gave a rumbling chuckle. Even more deadly?

Seeker tried to stand and managed, with the help of the gully wall, to come upright. The pain almost knocked the ursoid down again, but it gritted its teeth and hung on, closing its eyes against the spinning and nausea. Then it began to shuffle and limp down the gully. Three hills, it told itself. Only three. It began to climb the side of the gully.

A good hour later, it lay at the bottom of the last hill, sobbing for breath, too weak and exhausted to stand. No hope, it wailed silently, no hope. I can't make it all the way to Start before nightfall. I can't ever make it back. I'll die right here. The predators will be coming for me. The flyers, the things by the nest on the ridge.

It looked up with weary, blurred eyes and stared off south. Start is that way. The ridge was on the left, the stream on the right. Down that way. Down that way, then over the ridge to Start.

Once I would have done it in a flash. Once I was young and swift, the swiftest on the plain. I could run like the wind. Yes. And then . . . and then . . .

Seeker pulled itself out of old pain and back to the new. I won't quit. I won't be the first to die. Is all my pain to be for nothing? All the long years of suffering and doubt and fear? I was the first to see the plain rise up and up and up. The first to ask why. The first . . .

No. I must get up and move. There. Slowly, slowly. Stand. Now move. One foot. Another. Yes. One. Another. One. Another. But there is no hope. Labyrinth has killed me. Killed me first because I am the most unworthy. I chased useless things for the sheer joy of it. I asked for knowledge I had no right to. And even when they told me to stop, I kept on. One. Another.

Dimly Seeker wondered where Longarm was. The Teacher had said it would be out watching over them. Could the strange creature be somewhere nearby, watching, chuckling at Seeker's predicament, shaking its head in disgust at the stupidity of the Pretender? If you're out there, Longarm, Seeker silently pleaded, I need your help. You can laugh and sneer all you want, just come and help me.

But would the Teacher really help, even if it could? Or would it just stand by and hoot with laughter as Seeker died? The ursoid was profoundly unsure of exactly where Longarm stood, whether the creature was really there to help them or was in fact another trick of the planet, intended to confuse and ultimately to destroy them. Or perhaps the Teacher was something utterly different, something Seeker couldn't even imagine. But Longarm had nothing to do with the mess I'm in, Seeker admitted. It isn't the Teacher's fault that I am dying because I was foolish enough to tangle with that creature. . . .

Does death always come this way, in fear, in despair? Seeker wondered, its mind and body exhausted in a way that went beyond any weariness it had ever known or even imagined. I am utterly alone. No Nurturer will stand by me as I die and chant the Story to me. No one will breathe in my dead mouth to give me the Breath of Life so that I can return to the plain again and run and run as free as the wind. I am alone and death is my only companion.

But death is not a companion. Death is in me, around me, is me. This is my death. Mine alone. I cannot share it. One. Another. One. Another.

Dark. My sight is failing. I'm dying. No. I won't be the first. But the predators will come. One. Another. One. Another. There is no hope. Labyrinth will triumph, has triumphed. One. Another. Why not just lie down? The pain will be less. It will soon be over. There is no hope. No. One. Another. One. Another. One. Another.

VIII.

Longarm stared down. H*mb*l was behind the Teacher. The others were there on the side. Bilrog had a bandage around its head. Darkhider was scraped badly on its left side. Thisunit's robe was ripped and stained.

"Damn, you might not be smart, but you sure are tough!" Longarm chuckled. "What in the name of the Primordial Tree did you tackle with? An army?"

Seeker moaned and closed its eyes again. "Fear," it whispered in a soft growl, unable to speak more loudly. "You . . . right, Teacher. Fear is smartest. There is no hope. All alone. One. Another."

"Hey, you're back, Seeker. You made it. Came stumbling in here about an hour after dark. Cut to shit. Bleeding like a lunkworm. But you made it, Pretender. Damnedest thing I ever saw. How did you avoid the scavengers? You are without a doubt the luckiest Pretender I ever saw." Longarm continued to chatter as it carefully checked Seeker's wounds, cleaned them and put a gooey brown salve on them. "There. Patched up. In a week or so you'll be fine and ready to go out again."

Seeker's eyes opened slowly. "Go out again?" The ursoid shuddered with fear. "Out again? Out to death again, out to the things that are waiting. No hope, Longarm. You were right. Fear. Fear is best."

Bilrog cleared its throat. "Ahemmm, uh, don't worry, Seeker. We all, ummm, learned some hard lessons today. I, uh, don't think any of us will be going back out right away. Except maybe H*mb*l."

Thisunit nodded. "Bilrog's assessment is essentially correct. This unit plans to spend at least one day analyzing the results of the, uh, data it has collected on this first solo expedition onto the face of the planet."

"Darkhider will lay in itsss hole and lick itsss woundsss, yesss. Darkhider isss very frightened, Ssseeker."

Longarm laughed loudly. "Well, well, well! So my fine aggressive new Pretenders are beginning to understand! Wait, wait, the fun is only beginning. Now comes the second phase of Labyrinth's attack. The fear is set in motion. It will grow in you, take over your mind, turn you into a frightened, shivering thing. Yes, yes, now the attack is more subtle. I've seen Pretenders go crazy after a week of it. Crazy. They run screaming out of Start, trying to get back home on foot! They last maybe a mile or two. Then Labyrinth takes them!

"Weakness! There is no place for weakness on this planet.

And yet none of you even knows the strength that is needed. You will learn. Or you will die. Oh, yes." With another hoot of laughter, the Teacher turned away and went toward its quarters. "H*mb*l and Bilrog can help you to your shack, Seeker," it called back without turning. "Or you can get there on your own. You got this far. A little further won't hurt."

H*mb*l and Bilrog helped Seeker stand, but the ursoid waved them away when they tried to help further. "Longarm is right, I can make it the rest of the way alone." With nods and reassuring mumbles, the others dispersed through the dark to their own quarters. H*mb*l walked slowly by Seeker's side as the ursoid painfully dragged itself up the hill.

When they reached the shack, Seeker refused to go in. "It won't rain tonight. I . . . I want to stay out here." H*mb*l stood uncertainly, shifting its weight from foot to foot and buzzing worriedly. Seeker carefully lowered itself to a sitting position next to the door of the shack and stared up at the stars that blazed in the night sky. After hanging around for several moments as if to make sure Seeker was all right, H*mb*l buzzed a soft "good night" and went in. The ursoid nodded silent acknowledgement and turned its attention back to the stars.

So many, the Pretender thought. Here nearer to the Center, the stars cluster more thickly. And life is more common.

Life. How thin a thing it is. How slender the thread that keeps it from plummeting into the endless abyss of nothingness. And yet it is a strong thing, too. Tough enough to emerge again and again on world after world. How strange. One creature's life is so fragile, yet life itself is so strong.

Seeker heard a slight sound of movement off to the left. Fear welled up inside its throat and it sat rigidly, wondering if Labyrinth was reaching right into Start to take its life. Then from out of the dark a low, saurian form crept. Darkhider.

"Ah, Ssseeker," it addressed the ursoid. "I wasss hoping you would be awake. I . . . I want to talk with you. Would you be willing to . . ."

Seeker nodded, relief and annoyance flooding its mind at the same time. "Yes, Darkhider, I'd be happy for your company right about now. Was . . . was your day difficult?"

The saurian hissed in fear. "Yessss. Moressso than my wild-essst fantasssy. I lossst many ssscalesss and two of my mosssst

prissed amuletsss. It wasss only by the help of the Ssslime
Godsss that I essscaped at all. I fear, Ssseeker. I do not think
that I will sssurvive thisss dreadful planet."

"I'm not sure any of us will," Seeker responded, its voice
heavy with gloom. It told Darkhider what had happened to it,
of the three battles it had fought and how it had almost lost the
last one. "But the worst was getting back to Start," the ursoid
finished with a soft growl. It stopped speaking and gazed off at
the distant stars once more, its face troubled and its eyes dark
with emotion.

Finally it turned to Darkhider. "Why did you come here,
Darkhider? You . . . I mean, your race doesn't seem . . . I
mean . . ."

"Yesss, you are right. My rassse doesssn't ssseem like the
kind that would want to come to Labyrinth. We are jussst asss
Bilrog hasss sssaid, a rassse of cowardly lizzzardsss.

"We have sssurvived becaussse of our cowardisssse, Ssseeker. Our Godsss demand it. On my planet, flight is the
mossst acsssepted way of dealing with danger." Darkhider
sighed in a long hiss. "You sssee, we were only one of many
sssaurian ssspecies, and not the largessst, or fassstessst, or
mossst deadly by any meansss. There were many with long,
sssharp teeth and dreadful razzzorlike clawsss. From the very
moment the firssst of usss crawled from the Primordial Egg,
our only hope for sssurvival wasss to run and hide."

Darkhider paused and gave a furtive look around the area,
then moved closer to Seeker and spoke in a low, confidential
voice. "It isss sssaid that when the Ssslime Godsss firssst came
to our world, it wasss empty of life. There wasss nothing but
the originary ssslime and oozzze. But the Ssslime Godsss
sssaw it wasss a good world, ssso they plasssed the Primordial
Egg in the middle of the ssslime and all the creaturesss began
to hatch out. Two of the Ssslime Godsss, called Thinksss
Before and Thinksss After, were given the job of equipping
each creature with its powersss and abilitiesss. Thinksss After
begged to be allowed to do the work by itself. Thinksss Before
finally agreed and said it would check later to sssee that
everything had been done correctly.

"Ssso Thinksss After ssset to work. It gave sssome creaturesss ssstrength or long clawsss or sssharp teeth. To thossse that
were sssmaller and weaker, it gave ssspeed or wingsss or an

ability to burrow ssswiftly or sssome other ssskill that would allow them to ssstay alive. Thusss, Thinksss After took care of each creature asss it crawled from the Primordial Egg. It followed the great Law of Compensssation, balancing advantagesss and disssadvantagesss carefully ssso that no creature would be ssso weak asss to perisssh.

"But then, last of all, my rassse crawled from the Primordial Egg and ssssssss, there were no more powersss and abilitiesss left for usss! Thinksss After had usssed them all up! It called to Thinksss Before, wondering what to do. Thinksss Before pondered long and finally sssaid, 'We did not mean to give sssentiensssse to any of the creaturesss, for only the Ssslime Godsss have sssentiensssse. But there isss no choisssse now. If we do not give thessse poor creaturesss sssentiensssse, they will not sssurvive. Yet we cannot give them pure sssentiensssse or they will be asss godsss. Ssso we musssst mix it with sssomething even more wonderful. We musssst give them the greatesssst gift of all. We musssst give them fear. With intelligensssse and fear to bring it to life, they will sssurvive. Yessss.' And ssso it wasss done and we gained the greatesssst gift of all . . . fear.

"Fear, yesss, fear wasss what sssaved usss. Fear drove uss to be sssmarter than the othersss, fear made usss inventive, creative, clever, dangerousss. And ssso we prosssspered ssso much that we eventually came to be the only major ssspeciesss on our world. We, the cowardsss, the hidersss, the fleersss, became the rulersss. The fanged and clawed onesss, the huge and ssswift ones, died.

"Think of it, Sssseeker. A planet dominated by creaturesss who sssurvived becausssse they were afraid. Fear isss built into them ssso deeply that they cannot live without it. It isss the mosssst basssic truth in their exisssstensssse.

"And then sssuddenly, there isss nothing left to fear! They have won! They are the absssolute massstersss of the world! Isss thisss not wonderful? Do they not celebrate with endlesssss joy? Fear isss beaten! Fear isss no more!"

Darkhider paused and shivered, hunching down to the ground. "Yessss, oh, yesss. Fear isss gone. And ssso isss the one thing that drove our rassse onward, the mainssspring of our exisssstensssse. Fear, the thing that made usss what we were, wasss suddenly ussselessss, unnecessssary. And asss a resssult, we were adrift, lossst.

"Our very sssuccessss became our undoing. We began to fade. The number of fertile eggsss declined dramatically. Fewer and fewer of usss were born, and many of thossse were weak and sssickly. We tried to import horrorsss from other planetsss, dangerousss creaturesss that would hunt and kill usss. But they didn't adapt, they weren't interesssted in cowardly lizzzardsss, our flesssh was tassstelessss to them.

"We are a dying ssspeciesss, Ssseeker. We die for lack of fear. That isss why I am here on Labyrinth."

Seeker stared at the saurian. "You came here because this is the most fearsome place in the universe?"

"Yesss! I come to learn all there isss to know of fear! Perhapsss I can dissscover the sssecret of Labyrinth and bring sssome hope back to my people. If we could fear again . . ." Darkhider looked up at Seeker. "You knew fear today. Deeply, thoroughly. Isss it not wonderful? Can you undersssstand what it musst be like to be without it?"

"Then you didn't mind what happened to you today?" the ursoid asked, looking questioningly at the wounds on Darkhider's side.

The saurian shuddered. "I . . . I wasss deeply afraid. It . . . it did not feel good. I am worried, Ssseeker, that thisss plassse is too ssstrong for me, that the fear here isss tooo great. I do not know if I am ssstrong enough to withssstand it. And if I fail, then my people . . ." The words trailed off into the night.

Seeker nodded. "Yes. The fear is very strong. I am afraid now. I was so confident before, but now I'm not sure. I have seen death more closely than ever in my life. I do not like it. Yet I cannot give in to despair." The ursoid gestured up at the stars. "My people have a belief. When we die, one of our eyes goes into the earth, because that's where we came from. It lives there, quietly waiting. But the other eye goes into the heavens, from where it looks down at us and guards over us. Sometimes one of the eyes in the sky falls back to earth, where it rejoins the eye waiting there. When they come together, they form a new creature which is born again on the face of the planet. So when we look up at the sky at night, Darkhider, we say we are looking at ourselves. And the stars seem friendly and caring.

"But here on Labyrinth, the skies are all different. None of the stars are in the same places. They cannot be the eyes of those who went before us gazing down with kind benevolence. No, here they are cold and uncaring. And yet they are still so beautiful. Just as beautiful as they always were at home. How can that be? How can two such opposite things dwell together?"

Seeker paused and sighed. "But that isn't really so strange, is it? I despair, yet also I hope. I no longer know which is the most powerful of the two. I feel very, very mortal. And fragile."

"And yet you made it all the way back," Darkhider hissed softly, "ssso you are ssstrong and tough asss well, Ssseeker."

"Yes. Fragile and strong. How strange."

The two sat in companionable silence for a long time. Eventually, Darkhider slid away into the dark to find its hole for the night. Seeker didn't even notice when the saurian left.

What if everything in the world were a misunderstanding, what if laughter were really tears?

Soren Kierkegaard

❧❦❧

Swift strained its eyes as it gazed into the distance. Already my eyesight is dimming, it thought miserably. Already I lose the keen, far-seeing vision of a Chaser. It hunched its shoulders ever so slightly, curving its once straight back.

But even dimmer eyesight could not miss what the distance revealed. The plain rose up into the sky. It went up and up until it disappeared into the clouds. How many times have I come here, alone, to see this? Swift wondered sadly. How many times have I had to prove to myself that I was not wrong that day, that I had indeed seen what I had seen? Swift sighed and shook its head, then turned away and began to trot back toward where the pack would be gathering for the night.

How slowly I move! Swift thought. My limbs thicken, my claws grow, I gain weight. It felt the itching on its back. Yes, there was no denying it. The final protoegg was almost ripe. Soon some Catcher would harvest it. And then it would all be over.

Swift stopped in its tracks and moaned with dismay. How quickly it had all happened! When I told them what I had seen, they all laughed at me and scorned me as a fool and a useless one. You may be fast, they said, but your speed is wasted because you don't use it for the pack. You chase silly visions,

mirages, and creatures without enough meat to replenish the
energy spent in the chase. They did not understand the glory,
the beauty, the exhilaration of the chase, the wonder of the
thing Swift had seen. The plain rising up into the air! None had
even been willing to go and see it. A waste of time, they'd
said. We have game to chase and catch. Even Dreadclaw had
only looked sadly at Swift and shaken its head.

When the Nurturers heard of Swift's adventure, their reac-
tion was different. Knowever, the oldest Nurturer Swift had
ever seen, called Swift to it and demanded a full account of
what had happened. Eagerly, Swift explained, proud of its
discovery, proud of its speed and skill. Nothing was left out,
the flowers, the springdasher, the glidewing, the sun, the
clouds, the feel of the wind, the thrill of the chase and then the
plain, the plain reaching up and up and up . . . Swift had
been so sure that the Nurturer, one of the wisest on the plain
and the very one that had cared for it when it was a cub, would
understand its tale and praise it.

But that wasn't what happened at all. Knowever listened
carefully, silently, asking for occasional clarifications or ex-
pansions. Then, equally silently, its brow furrowed with a
frown, the Nurturer turned away and waddled off.

Two pawfuls of days later, three new Nurturers had shown
up in the midst of Swift's pack. None of the Chasers or
Catchers had ever seen these new ones. They were very old and
powerful-looking, their eyes deep and dark with heavy wisdom
and many years of nurturing. They smelled strangely of things
no one could identify. There was an air of . . .Swift had
struggled to find a word and suddenly it had arrived . . . there
was an air of "beyond" about them. Swift shivered with a
mixture of excitement and terror when it first laid eyes on
them.

They quizzed Swift closely. Once more the Chaser related its
tale, leaving nothing out. It didn't merely tell the story drily,
simply reciting dull facts. No, it relived the event, recollecting
the feelings, the wonder, the joy, the power, the wind and the
sun and the springdasher and the plain going up and up and
up . . .

When Swift was finished, the strange Nurturers had gone off
by themselves and spent many hours talking softly with each
other. Then they returned and surrounded the Chaser. The

oldest, a huge creature with silvered and grizzled fur, admonished Swift softly and at great length. You should not go so far from your pack, it remonstrated. You should not chase useless things. You should not go to the east, for strange things happen there. You were mistaken, your eyes played you a trick, you did not see the plain going up and up and up. Then they gave the Chaser something to drink. It had been foul-smelling and bitter, but when Nurturers demand, Chasers must obey. Swift drank the horrid stuff, and it burned all the way down. The Chaser was sick for two days.

Then it began to happen. The most horrible thing began to happen. Swift's second protoegg matured. And quickly on its heels, the third. Dreadclaw harvested the second. Which was fine, for Swift liked Dreadclaw. The Catcher was gentle and understanding. It had even listened with a half-smile, curving its muzzle, when Swift told of the plain.

But the third. Ah, the third! Crusharm grabbed Swift unexpectedly, before the protoegg was even fully ready. Grabbed Swift and literally ripped the protoegg from its pouch. When Swift tried to resist, Crusharm slammed the Chaser into the ground with a mighty blow. And then beat Swift senseless. And ripped the protoegg . . .

For days, Swift stayed away from the pack, dreading their growls of contempt, their sneering looks, their disdain. And the fourth pouch began to itch.

Impossible! It took years for a Chaser to mature all its protoeggs. Years! All that time they ran free, chasing the game, feeling the wind in their hair, skimming along the ground, almost flying. The glory of it! And Swift was the fastest on the plain, the best!

The fourth protoegg matured. Swift's limbs thickened. It gained weight, lost speed. Lost speed! What was there left to live for? If it was never to run again, never to leap and prance around the game, driving it . . . If all that was left was the slow power of the Catcher . . . Was everything just a lie, just a foolish misunderstanding?

Crusharm took the fourth egg, too. Swift fell into bitter despair. It went off by itself, away from the pack, to die. It moved slowly, sadly across the plain, heading, without even noticing, toward the place where the sun rose. On and on it went, drawn by some strange longing. On and on, past the usual hunting grounds of the pack, out further and further until . . .

The plain rose into the sky.

And the wonder filled it once again. The beauty of it, the sheer glory of the plain rising into the sky. Up and up and up until even the glidewings would have trouble reaching it. This thing could not be evil, could not be bad, could not even be an illusion or a mistake. No, there was no lie here, no misunderstanding. And suddenly Swift was filled with an inexplicable longing to go and follow the plain up into the sky, to look down on the world, down on the glidewings, the pack, the Nurturers, the clouds . . . Swift took a step toward the wonder it saw in the east. Took a step and then stopped.

A sudden light flooded Swift's mind, and the Chaser made the connection. I saw the plain rising into the sky and told the pack. The Nurturers came and questioned me. They gave me something to drink. And I changed.

They did this to me! They changed me! Why? Why?

Because I saw the plain rising into the sky.

Why?

And Swift decided not to die after all. Because it wanted to know why.

Swift flexed its claws, gazing at them with wonder and dismay. I am almost a Catcher, it thought. Only this last egg to go and I will finish the process. Then I will spend most of my time with the pack, waiting for the Chasers to bring the game in so I can grab and kill it as they drive it by. It flexed its growing muscles. How different its body felt! The leanness, the lightness, the blinding speed were gone forever. Now there was power and speed of a different sort.

Will I be as strong a Catcher as I was swift a Chaser? Will I still be the best on the plain? Swift growled softly at the thought. I shall call myself Strong. And if Crusharm comes within my grasp, I will give it the thrashing of its life.

And will I ever go to see the plain rising into the sky again? Yes! Swift declared passionately. Yes! They have changed me because of what I saw! I will see it again and again! I will force them to come and tell me why, why the plain does what it does and why they changed me! Something has happened here, something very important, something even the Nurturers don't tell us of when they raise us. There is a secret here, a mystery tc be solved. The plain goes up into the sky. I did not imagine it. I will force them to admit that it is true, force them to acknowledge that I was right. If the old ones come again, and I will make them come, I will grab them with my powerful paws and threaten them with my sharp claws and I will force the truth from them.

The creature growled deeply. No, this is not over yet. They have done things to me, tried to stop me, but this is not over yet. They think they have won by turning me into a Catcher. But they are wrong, for I have not forgotten what I have seen and what they have done. Swift is dead. But I am Strong, the most powerful Catcher on the plain, and I will force them!

Growling and muttering to itself, Strong strode across the plain heading for the pack.

Dialectical Dances

We come to terms with the question of existence always only through existence itself.

Martin Heidegger

The trick was to dodge in under the horns and eviscerate the creature with one deft swipe of the claws. The problem was that if the first attempt failed, there was no second chance, for the beast was too intelligent to fall for the same trick again. And, once wounded, it was more dangerous than ever.

Strong gave a quick glance over its shoulder. The other Catchers had backed away. Afraid? Or just hoping I'll fail and get hooked on one of the horns? Probably both.

The Catcher turned its attention back to the hornhead which three of the Chasers were driving swiftly across the plain toward the pack. No telling how far they had run the beast, but it didn't really matter. Hornheads could run all day and still put up a terrific and deadly fight.

The Chasers saw that Strong was in position to catch and signaled to let the Catcher know they were driving the beast in its direction. Strong signaled back and got ready.

Strong flexed its knees slightly and turned directly into the line of the hornhead's approach. The Catcher's broad body made a good-sized target. But the left foot was slightly forward, the right slightly back, and the torso twisted to the left at the waist, tightly coiled like a spring. The left arm was back and down, claws facing outward. The right was slightly out, making the target appear even wider than it was.

The hornhead was close now, close enough to see . . . Ah! The beast spotted Strong and gave a bellow. Here at last was something to attack! Something that stood still and didn't dart away whenever the beast swung its head. With a snort, the hornhead lowered its head and charged the Catcher.

Strong relaxed every muscle in its body as the beast thundered toward it. No tension now. Softness and flexibility were the key. The monster, its head bristling with three pairs of razor-sharp horns, aimed itself at the Catcher and lunged forward. It looked as if there was no hope for the motionless creature that stood and stood and stood and . . .

As the horns swept toward Strong's right side, the Catcher caught one with the claws of its right hand. At the same instant, using the force of the beast's charge, Strong twisted its body to the right, allowing the horns to pass by its stomach with less than an inch to spare. As it turned, it dropped down, its left arm striking around in a sweep, the claw extended, catching the hornhead low in the side, just below where its ribs ended. The sound of the claws ripping through flesh could be heard fifteen feet away.

The hornhead bellowed with pain as it roared past Strong. Then, faster than such a huge animal should be able to move, it spun around and prepared to attack again. A moaning growl went up from the watching Catchers and Chasers. Strong stood tall and straight, looking intently into the beast's eyes.

It opened its mouth to bellow a challenge before it charged and hot blood came spewing out. Dismay filled its eyes. Then rage. It stepped forward, making the first move to charge . . . and its front legs buckled. From its right side there suddenly burst forth a gush of blood and intestines. With a gurgle, the hornhead crumpled to the ground, its eyes glazing in death.

A roar came welling out of Strong's throat. It held its clawed hands to the sky and shook them as if in defiance of some celestial onlookers. Behind it, the other Catchers and Chasers growled their respect and pleasure.

All except one. Crusharm. The older, larger, possibly even stronger Catcher snarled in derision and anger. "You haven't changed from your days as a Chaser, Strong! Still a fool who takes unnecessary chances and is more concerned with its own welfare than with that of the pack!"

Strong turned calmly and looked coldly at Crusharm. "The kill was not clean enough for you? Not swift enough? You think that you could have done better?"

"It was clean and swift enough for a beginner. And yes, I could have done better. But that is not what I object to, and you know it well, Strong."

"Ah, then why not say it that all might hear, Crusharm, taker of eggs, killer of the weak and old?"

Crusharm's fur rose and its crest flared up at the cool insolence and disrespect of Strong's reply. With an effort, the Catcher controlled its temper and spoke in a voice choked with fury. "You tempt the Chasers to chase dangerous game, worthless game, even as you did when you were a Chaser. There was no need to attempt a catch on a hornhead and you know it. You sent them out for one, don't deny it. There is safer game to be had. Your folly endangers the pack. Just as it did when you were a Chaser!"

Strong sneered a low growl at Crusharm. "Yes, I sent them! Hornhead meat is delicious. And I am not afraid to catch one driven to me! I do not cower back with the old and the weak, with the fat and slow ones whose protoeggs are almost all gone, taken by Nurturers! I am Strong, the quickest, strongest, most deadly Catcher on the plain! Just as I was once Swift, the fastest Chaser that ever lived! And you are Crusharm, a fool, an egg taker, a carrion catcher!"

Taunted past endurance by Strong's attitude and words, Crusharm gave a roar of fury and threw itself at the other Catcher. Strong stepped quickly back and to the left, evading Crusharm's first blow, the one meant to end it all, and slashed the huge Catcher across the ribs.

Crusharm spun instantly and caught Strong across the forearm with a slashing attack that spewed blood and bits of flesh into the air. Strong stepped back and the two of them stood face to face, growling and breathing heavily. "I will kill you," Crusharm muttered so softly only Strong could hear.

Strong growled gently in reply. "I think not, old one. I have watched you for many seasons now. You are slow. Strong, but slow. I am faster. I will cut you to ribbons. Think of the eggs you tore from my pouches and the beatings you gave me.

Think of them and know fear, for I am about to avenge them."

With a roar, Crusharm lunged forward. Strong stepped slightly to the left side and raked swift claws down its opponent's left arm. Crusharm turned in that direction, striking out with its right arm, but Strong ducked down almost to the ground as it wove back out of the way while its own right arm swept out and slashed the back of Crusharm's.

Again and again, Crusharm struck out at Strong and each time the younger Catcher stepped out of the way at the last instant and raked its claws across the arm that tried to hit it. Soon Crusharm's arms were streaming blood, and bits of flesh hung in strips from them. It was becoming apparent to all those watching that Crusharm was finding it difficult to lift its arms to attack.

Then Strong changed tactics. With its opponent's arms so badly injured as to be almost useless, it was virtually weaponless. Strong struck, raking blood-dripping claws across the side of Crusharm's face, ripping its ear off and nearly hitting an eye. Crusharm tried to block, but its arms wouldn't move swiftly enough. Slash after slash hit home until Crusharm was staggering and moaning, the blood matting its fur.

Strong roared in triumph and was about to step in for the kill when a huge voice stopped both fighters dead in their tracks. "Stop this fighting instantly!" Surprised, Strong turned to face Knowever. "Stop it, I say!"

Growling softly, Strong stepped back and gave way to Knowever as the Nurturer waddled between the two Catchers. Knowever looked Crusharm up and down, then gave Strong a similar going-over. "Fools!" the Nurturer roared. "Damn stupid fools! I raised both of you! Your eggs came from my pouches! I suckled you and whispered things in your ears! Did neither of you two ever hear any of the things I taught you when you were cubs? We do not fight each other! We never fight each other! Our claws, our teeth are for the game, to catch and kill the game, not to harm each other! This is one of the most basic lessons of cubhood!"

Growling softly, Knowever examined Crusharm while Strong stood meekly by. "Damn good thing I got here. You've just about killed this Chaser, Strong. Just about killed one of your own."

"Crusharm is not one of my own. Crusharm is my enemy."

Knowever whirled on Strong with a snarl of anger. "Enemy? Not one of your own? Where do these words come from? These are empty words that do not apply to Chasers or Catchers or Nurturers. We are all one. Chaser, Catcher, Nurturer. Each and every one of us has been or will be all three. So we are one. All one."

"I am not one with Crusharm."

Knowever scowled. "You are one. Say it, admit it. You are one with Crusharm!"

Strong drew itself up. "I am Strong. I have seen the plain rise into the sky! I am one with no one but myself, for no one else has seen what I have seen."

"No," Knowever declared, "no one is by itself. We are all part of the pack. We can have no identity apart from the pack. We live and die for the pack. Chasers chase game for the sake of the pack. Catchers catch game for the sake of the pack. And Nurturers nurture the cubs so that the pack might continue.

"You," Knowever continued with a slight sneer, "you claim you have seen these things that even the wisest and oldest Nurturers deny can be seen. You claim to have this secret, this vision of what is impossible. There can be no secrets in the pack. Everything must be open. The law of the pack demands it."

"But I have seen these things!" Strong protested. "I have! And I can show them to you, take you to see them with your own eyes. Come, I dare you, come!"

"There is no need to waste the time of the pack in such foolish pursuits. The oldest Nurturers say such a thing cannot be. There is no tale in pack lore that tells of such a thing. None of the others in the pack have seen this thing. You must cease claiming such a thing exists."

"I tell you it does! The plain rises up into the sky!"

"SILENCE!" Knowever roared so loudly that Strong stepped back in dismay. "The laws of the pack do not allow for such a thing! You try to suspend the laws of the pack for your own fantastic visions, try to force all of us to accept your delusions. And see where such conduct leads you?" Knowever gestured grandly toward the bleeding form of Crusharm. "You break yet another law and use your claws and teeth against one of your own. This cannot be allowed to continue. You must renounce your foolish claims." Knowever drew itself up to its full height. "You must renounce your foolish claims if you wish to stay in the pack."

The Nurturer's final words stunned Strong. Was Knowever threatening to chase Strong from the pack, to exile the Catcher? Strong had never known such a thing to happen, but there were legends of it. Every cub heard them and trembled with fear at the very idea. No one could live without the pack. Chasers could chase but not catch. Catchers could catch but not chase. And Nurturers could do neither. Any one of them alone was helpless and doomed to death by starvation.

Worse yet, an exile would be alone! All its life, Strong had been surrounded by the pack. Even though the Catcher had often rebelled against the pack and gone off on its own for short periods, it had always come back. The pack was life. The pack was the real, the solid, the actual. Without the pack a Chaser or a Catcher or even a Nurturer was only a partial creature, a mere possibility. The pack gave life substance, shape, meaning.

And yet, and yet . . . the pack also limited possibility. If one stayed with the pack, one could only become what the pack said one could become. Strong had never had this thought before. It shook the Chaser deeply. Were there things to be other than a Chaser or a Catcher or a Nurturer? And if so, what in the world could they be? Strong's mind sheered away from the question, frightened by the size of it. The Catcher shivered as if suddenly cold, and swayed slightly as if a strong wind were blowing it. Exile. Sent away from the pack to die because of what it had seen. And yet it had seen it, had seen it many times. Strong swallowed a lump that had appeared in its throat. The Catcher had to speak, had to say what it knew. "But . . . but I saw it. I have seen it again and again. I go there and it is still there. I . . . ."

"This is impossible. It cannot be. You are mistaken."

"But I . . . ."

"ENOUGH!" Knowever roared again. "I will hear no more! You will speak no more! I will call on the Council, as I did when you first came back from the east with this lie in your mouth. Since you will not pay me heed, perhaps you will listen to the wisdom of the Council. And if not, then they have ways of making you listen!" With that, Knowever turned away from Strong and began to minister to Crusharm's wounds.

For several moments, Strong stood stupidly and watched. Then, slowly, the Catcher turned and wandered over to where the dead hornhead lay. It was a good kill, a clean kill, Strong thought dully. Worthy of praise. Worthy of . . .

The Catcher looked up into the sky. A lone glidewing hovered there, far off beyond the scattered clouds that dotted the blue. As so often before, Strong's heart went out to the glidewing, wishing with all its might that it might take off and soar with the creature, high, high, high above the plain, high above all the pain and confusion and lies.

I have seen it! I have! And nothing they can say or do will change that, Strong reassured itself. Why do they refuse to admit what I know to be true? Why do they try to force me to believe as they do, to believe against what I have seen with my own eyes?

And why, why, why does the plain rise into the sky?

Not seeing or hearing any of the other members of the pack, Strong began to walk off across the plain. Off toward the east, where the sun rose every morning.

Language fails, and thought is confounded; for who is happiest, except the unhappiest, and who the unhappiest, except the happiest, and what is life but madness, and faith but folly, and hope but the briefest respite, and love but vinegar in the wound.

Soren Kierkegaard

I.

Just a few more bits of data and the pattern would be complete. Thisunit was sure of it, to a least a three-sigma level of confidence. And yet . . . there was a vague sense of discomfort over the patterns that seemed to be emerging.

No. That didn't compute. Not discomfort. The pattern was almost complete. That was the problem. Incomplete patterns were always uncomfortable. That tiny remaining gap that had to be closed was always a source of worry.

The gap. Yes. That was the source of the discomfort. The gap that had been there and still remained. Thisunit knew approximately the kind of data needed to fill it. Indeed, the creature's last few journeys out onto the surface of Labyrinth had been solely in search of that data. And several times, Thisunit had been sure it had found the needed information.

But each time something strange had happened. When the data had been fed into the model Thisunit had constructed from the other information (a highly complex and comprehensive model, perhaps, Thisunit estimated, one of the greatest ever built), something had always shifted just slightly and the gap had opened again someplace new. The first few times this had happened, Thisunit had simply sighed with frustration and gone out again to gain the new final information. But now

Thisunit was beginning to wonder. How long would these shifts continue to take place?

A thought came, one that had to be immediately suppressed, but which instantly crept back into consciousness. What if the approximation process was infinite? What if the regression went on forever? What if every new bit of data subtly transformed every old bit and shifted the pattern just enough to open new gaps?

No. Such a thing could not be. There was always a way to close a system. To complete it so that it was self-consistent. Start with the correct premises and work the details out. It was simple and automatic. Then check the structure against the reality and see where the correspondences were off. Readjust the model for the deviations, and everything became certain.

Oh, there was randomness in the universe. It was hard to tell which atom would decay when. Hard, but not impossible. There was a model that gave very good results, at least in the aggregate. And, after all, the model Thisunit was constructing for Labyrinth was similar in that it took many variables into account and tried for statistical certainty.

And yet . . . Was statistical certainty certain enough where a being's life was at stake? For that was the actual situation on Labyrinth. If the model was off by a few percentage points, the result wouldn't just be a minor break-down in prediction. It could well result in death for an unwary individual.

Several times now Thisunit had almost been destroyed in areas it was sure it understood. They were areas that had been thoroughly mapped and explored. All the patterns had been studied and placed in context. And then they shifted, suddenly, unexpectedly, and almost lethally. Creatures that had been relatively harmless alone came at Thisunit in a group, and the robed explorer had almost been destroyed. It had managed to kill the creatures and limp back to Start. Longarm had hooted with hilarity and badgered it endlessly about logic and foolishness.

The gap would close, the system would be completed. Thisunit was confident, knew it would be so. And yet . . . and yet . . .

II.

H*mb*1 stood and swayed slightly, unsure. Something was wrong, out of rhythm, jarring, cacophonous. Yes. There, that dark area off to the left. It vibrated at a different frequency, one that indicated hunger. Hunger. And H*mb*1 was food. How to avoid it? Go back the way it had come, back toward Start? No, no, that wasn't right, wasn't harmonious. This was the right movement, the right way to go, there was a feeling here of a sense of rhythm.

Hmmmmmmmm, H*mb*1 buzzed softly. Hmmmm-mmmm, yes. The creature swayed and twirled slightly, dipping its head, its right leg thrusting slowly out. Yes. Move with it, flow past it, yes.

See now it sways, too, following the rhythm, hmmm-mmmmm, yes, sways and dips and moves. We are dance partners, yes, bob and weave and twirl and spin. Hmmm-mmmmm. Hunger from it. So sad. It is hungry. Hmmm-mmmmm. Yes. There is a thing over here, over this way, a proper thing to hunt and eat. Yes. It follows, moving, sway-ing, following the natural beat, the proper flow.

Now past it as it scurries off after its prey. Yes. Hmm-mmmm. This is good. Farewell, dark thing. We have danced well together.

There are so many dances to be danced here on Labyrinth. So many and so varied. Some are dangerous. Some, perhaps, are deadly. To dance them well is joy. For this world is complete and full of wonder, and all is connected with all. There have been no interlopers here. Life is one.

Except for us. Yes, we are the interlopers, the disturbers. Should we be? No wonder Labyrinth tries to kill us. We disturb its harmony. Is it wrong for us to be here?

Ah, a new dance. This is one I have never danced before. A dangerous one. Yes. Hmmmmmmm. The creature has eight legs, strange rhythms, odd beats. There are patterns within patterns, some very alien even for Labyrinth. Move, yes, sway, yes. Hmmmmmmm. Approach, retreat, circle, recircle. Hard to match, hard to follow. Let the mind go, just move with it. It is right, I am wrong. Let go of "I," just be a pattern of movement, flow with the pattern, don't exist, don't be separate, merge, flow . . .

Spin! Leap back! Too late! Pain! Fiery anguish! Ah! Ah!
Struggle and twist! Break free! Run! Panic! No! No!

III.

Wounds on the body heal. Wounds on the mind . . . do they
heal as well? What of memory? Does it ever release one? Will
I ever be rid of the sight of the plain rising up to meet the sky?
Do I ever want to be?

There is pain in every memory because even if it is of good
times, it is of times past and gone forever. There can be no
calling back of what was, not even any repeating. No, once
gone, gone forever.

And yet the echoes hang on and on and on. And the memory
returns to pull the mind from now into then.

Seeker shook its head and looked at the hills. Shall I go to
the right or left and avoid them? Are there more creatures like
that which I fought and killed lurking in the gullies? Will I be
as lucky the second time?

The ursoid sighed and turned left, skirting the edge of the
hills. Fear dwells there to my right, it thought as it jogged
slowly along. Fear I am not yet ready to face again.

Longarm is right. Fear is proper here on Labyrinth. Seeker
snorted. Fear is proper anywhere. Labyrinth is deadly, but so
is life. No one ever gets out of it alive. The ursoid growled a
slight chuckle. Clever. Hmmmm. I must tell Longarm that
one. Life. No one gets out of it alive. Yes.

But how far should one's fear go? Here on Labyrinth, it is all
too easy to let fear get the upper hand and sit cowering in Start
for all time. And even that won't save you because Labyrinth
simply creeps into your mind and destroys you a different way.

Seeker remembered what it had been like while it had been
recuperating from its wounds. The depression had been very
deep and powerful. At first the ursoid had almost yielded to it,
had almost given up and decided to quit, to die right there
outside its shack, leaning against the rough wall, gazing up at
the stars.

But Longarm had scoffed and railed and joked and scolded

and humored and nagged and generally forced Seeker back to health and sanity and out onto the face of the planet again. This was now the third trip. The first two had been tentative and frightened and short. This one would be longer and more taxing.

And, it went without saying, more dangerous. There had already been two attacks, both easily handled. The flying things, and a creature about the size of a large dog. Confidence was returning.

The other Pretenders were having problems, too. Only Seeker had been badly mauled so far, but Darkhider had been unable to go out for two days, it had been so frightened. And even brave Bilrog moved like a hunted creature.

Ah. There, off to the left. What was that thing? Seeker stopped and stared. It was H*mb*1, all wrapped in white stuff and hanging in a tree! Seeker looked around carefully, trying to find any lurking beasts. Nothing.

Slowly, hesitantly, the ursoid approached the tree and H*mb*1. The creature seemed to be alive but was bound with something that looked like . . . Seeker reached out a hand and touched the white material that swathed H*mb*1. The ursoid shuddered and took an involuntary step back. It was! It was webbing!

Were there spiders here on Labyrinth as well? A piece of information lit up at the back of the ursoid's mind. Arachnids were present on every known world in the Federation. Seeker growled softly in wonder as it gazed at H*mb*1. Imagine the size of the spider that had been able to attack, subdue, and then hang a creature the size of H*mb*1 in this tree.

The hair on Seeker's back rose in sudden fear and its comb stood up stiff and red. The spider had to be huge. Huge and very dangerous. Seeker looked over its shoulders in apprehension. Was it near? Surely it had hung H*mb*1 here to keep for future use. Was it coming back? Was it on its way right this instant?

Seeker fought down its panic. No spider was in sight. Should it free H*mb*1? Was the creature already dead? It reached out a hand and touched the strange dancer. Warm to the touch. Not dead. Poisoned, drugged, but still alive.

The ursoid fought down a sudden surge of fear. It wanted to run away from here as fast as possible. Spiders! Huge ones!

Everything in its mind screamed for flight. But it couldn't just run off and leave H*mb*1 to sure death.

Why not? a part of it gibbered. Run, save yourself! Let the thing have H*mb*1. Then it won't want you!

Seeker shook its head in anger at the coward in its mind. H*mb*1 is my only friend. It is my pack. I must save it. The ursoid leaned forward and, with its knife, carefully cut H*mb*1 loose. Its hands were shaking the entire time, and it couldn't help glancing repeatedly over its shoulders to see if the spider was coming back for its prey.

Finally, H*mb*1 lay slumped on the ground, free of the webbing. Seeker lifted the limp form to its shoulders and began to carry it back toward Start. Every step was filled with dread and fear and sideward and backward glances.

It seemed to take forever, but just as dusk was falling, an exhausted Seeker dumped the still unconscious H*mb*1 in front of Longarm's door and bellowed for the Teacher to come and help him save the strange dancer.

IV.

Hiding, skulking, dashing furtively from cover to cover, that was the way. Those other fools, they marched right out in the open, right where every dangerous predator could see them. Not Darkhider, no. That was not the way of its people, not the way the sacred Gods of the Slime meant things to be. No.

That furry one, that Seeker. It liked that one. That one understood fear, even though it was big and strong. Darkhider shivered with pleasure. Fear. The chill of horror. Yes. The teeth closing on air just behind one's tail.

But that Seeker was a good one. It had seen it take H*mb*1 down from the tree. Darkhider itself had watched while H*mb*1 had danced with the spider and had seen the spider attack and bite and bind the dancer. When the spider had left, it had crept up and sat beneath H*mb*1, looking up helplessly. There was nothing it could do. Nothing but savor the horror of the situation.

Now it was hiding from a big thing with sharp claws and sharp teeth. Teeth that had closed on air just behind one's tail. Fear. Yes, fear and quickness and cleverness. There was always a hole nearby, a place to run and burrow and hide. It could hear the thing snuffling at the opening of the hole. Darkhider itself had dug this hole the last time it had been out. A place to retreat to in just such an emergency. It had several such hidey-holes in the area. Everytime it went out and went further from Start, it dug new holes, new places for escape.

The toothy thing was starting to dig now. Dig with big, sharp claws. Flesh-rending claws. Fear. A shiver of ecstasy. Darkhider reached down and took one of the fetishes from its belt. It began to hiss a hymn to the Slime God who had given him this particular fetish, this piece of its own power. When then the fetish began to warm up, when the god-power was swelling in it, Darkhider pointed it at the toothy one and spoke the word that released the god's anger. The toothy one died.

Darkhider crept out of its hole and looked around. Yes. It would survive. It would find its way to Sanctuary. It had to, or its race would die.

What it had told Seeker wasn't completely true. Darkhider was here not merely to learn of fear and find a solution to the dilemma of its race. No. Darkhider was here to scout this planet for its species. For there was only one solution to their problem, and they well knew it. They had to leave their home world. And where else in the universe could they come but to Labyrinth, one of the few worlds without a sentient species that would reject them . . . and the one place where they would always be afraid? Here they would flourish once more, their eggs would be fertile and their numbers grow.

Of course, that meant that the others could not be allowed to reach Sanctuary. Only Darkhider could be allowed to succeed. Only Darkhider could be allowed to survive. Labyrinth would probably do the job for it. Almost had with both Seeker and H*mb*1. But Darkhider would have to follow the others constantly, making sure they did not find Sanctuary. If they beat the planet, then it would have to step in when they least expected it and act. Yes. This world was destined to be his and his species'. They needed it. All the others had to die. Yes.

V.

Bilrog's knife slashed the thing along the side. It bellowed and leapt back. The Furmorian shouted its warcry and leapt forward, its weapon moving in a blur of death. There was a howl of pain, a gurgle, and then silence. Bilrog stood back and growled with pleasure. Dead. Another one dead.

And yet . . . a small voice deep within the warrior's mind whispered. And yet nothing! Bilrog shouted back. And yet can you kill them all, every one of them? the voice continued, ignoring the warrior's protests. I can. I will.

This dialogue is foolish, craven, not worthy of a Furmorian, Bilrog told itself. I am a warrior, a mighty warrior, the mightiest ever to stride the galaxy. I have killed creatures on a hundred worlds. With guns and arrows and spears and knives and my bare hands. There is no one as mighty as I!

But this time you fight a planet, the voice insisted.

And so this is my greatest fight! My song will be sung as long as warriors exist.

You will pass from the minds of beings, unknown, unsung, unmourned.

Bilrog howled with fury. NO! NO! YOU LIE!

Lie? I cannot lie.

The Furmorian leapt on the carcass of the creature it had slain, its knife slashing with rage. It hacked and cut, blood and flesh fountaining out around it. Panting, howling, moaning, it mangled the carcass beyond recognition. Then it leapt to its feet and began to run, its eyes haunted, its mind a haze of blood lust. A haze behind which a quiet voice waited for its chance to speak.

Something appeared ahead. Bilrog didn't even bother to study it. The warrior screamed out its warcry and flung itself on the creature.

Again the knife flashed and ripped. But the thing had weapons of its own. Sharp claws and powerful muscles. Long teeth and strong jaws. It fought back, roaring its own fury.

One pawful of claws smashed into the side of Bilrog's head and sent the warrior reeling. It leapt to its feet and paused to gauge its opponent more coolly. The thing was easily as tall as the Furmorian and much thicker across. It snarled and waved sharp, blood-covered claws at the warrior.

Bilrog looked down at its own body. There was blood all over it. Blood and loose pieces of its own flesh. It was wounded, and badly. But the voice was silent.

Slowly, carefully, it stalked around its opponent, eyeing it carefully, looking for an opening. There! It leapt forward, dodged the sweep of the clawed paw and drove its knife deep into the thing's gut. Then it ripped the blade sideways and threw itself back out of reach of the slashing teeth.

Again it leapt in and stabbed the creature. Bilrog felt itself slowing down. It had lost a good deal of blood and had several very serious wounds. But nothing fatal, it told itself. Not yet.

This was true combat, glorious striving against a worthy opponent. Bilrog roared and attacked. The paw caught the right shoulder and flung the Furmorian sideways. The knife, which Bilrog had stuck deep into the thing's gut, was torn from the warrior's grasp.

Bilrog hit the ground with a thump and rolled as swiftly as it could to gain distance from its opponent. Bilrog got slowly to its feet, both hands empty. The creature was looking at the warrior, waiting for the next assault. Bilrog could see the knife jutting from the creature's side.

For several moments it was a standoff. Then, unexpectedly, the creature turned to leave. It took two steps, hesitated, and finally crumpled to the ground with a bubbling sigh.

At first, Bilrog was too stunned to move. It was over. Unexpectedly, suddenly, finally. Cautiously, the warrior approached the bulk of its fallen opponent. Gently, with a foot, it prodded the creature. There was no response. Victory.

Bilrog sat down weakly on the carcass. Victory. Why do I feel so empty? It leaned over and pulled its weapon free, wiping it absently on the thing's fur.

The warrior stood, swaying slightly with fatigue and faintness. Another one. I've killed another one. Why do I feel so . . . so empty? I've killed another one. And yet . . .

VI.

Longarm shook its head. "H*mb*1 will live, Seeker. But it won't dance for a while. Did you see this spider?"

Seeker shook its head. "No. Only H*mb*1. Why?"

"Well, it's the first I've ever heard of it. No one's ever run into such a thing before that I know of. Interesting. Labyrinth keeps thinking up new things."

"But arachnids are common throughout the galaxy. They . . ."

"I know, I know. There's even a species of sentient arachnids. Two, actually, though one is so strange that contact has been impossible up to now. And there are arachnids here as on every planet. But one this size . . . Well, I've never heard of it, that's all. I wonder if it's the only one, or if there are others?"

Seeker shuddered. "I hope only one. Though that doesn't seem likely, does it?"

Longarm snorted. "Nothing seems likely here. But everything is. On Labyrinth, Seeker, every possibility is an actuality. Including, or perhaps I should say specifically, your own death."

"And my own life."

"Yes, that too. And your failure and your success."

"Success. Yes. Finding Sanctuary. And then . . ."

"And then spending the rest of your life finding it again and again and again, endlessly until finally Labyrinth gets you."

Seeker looked confused. "But I thought once you found Sanctuary, you were safe. That you . . ."

"Safe? Seeker, once you set foot on Labyrinth, it gets inside you. It's always there waiting, hoping, lurking, ready to strike out where and when you least expect it. There is no 'safe' for you any longer. Not for you or any of the others. You left 'safe' behind on your home world. Now you belong to Labyrinth."

"But . . . but what does it mean to be a Questioner, then?"

Longarm shrugged. "Not much. I guess all it really means is that you get the chance to leave Labyrinth and carry on your battle with it all across the face of the galaxy. Same fight, different places, that's all."

"But that makes no sense!"

"On the contrary, it makes all the sense in the world. This world, that is."

H*mb*1 moaned softly. Longarm nodded. "Coming back. Poison wasn't to kill, only to numb. This spider, like all the rest, likes its food fresh. It was just storing H*mb*1 until it was ready to eat it. Lucky you found your friend when you did."

"Longarm," Seeker said humbly, "I'm very confused."

The Teacher nodded. "Good. Shows you're making progress."

"But can't you just explain . . ."

Longarm hooted a laugh. "Explain? Is that how you think things are figured out? By explaining them? Come now, Seeker, you've lived long enough to know that isn't true. You sound like Thisunit with all its data and nonsense."

"But why is it nonsense to try and find an explanation?"

"Because an explanation is in words, objective things, limited, bound in time and place. And what you seek can't be so bound."

"But surely words can approach it."

"No." Longarm shook its shaggy head firmly. "Not directly, in any case. And is a mere approach really good enough? The issue is life and death here on Labyrinth. Is something approaching life, almost as good as life, almost certain, good enough? Will it save you to be almost alive? I think not."

"But if Thisunit's system approaches certainty to the tenth decimal place, surely that will be close enough."

Longarm laughed again. "And what if the next piece of data contradicts all the others? What if that eleventh decimal point is the only one that really matters? What if data and decimal points aren't the real issues at all? No, Seeker, Thisunit seeks objective certainty. The only thing possible objectively is probability, not certainty. And I can promise you one thing, if nothing else. Probability isn't going to get you to Sanctuary."

"Then what is?"

Longarm shrugged as it turned to re-enter its shack. "Damned if I know, Seeker. Damned if I know."

VII.

They ate their evening meal in silence, each wrapped in its own private thoughts. Bilrog had been the last to limp in, badly wounded. Longarm had grumped and grumbled the entire time while ministering to the warrior's wounds.

Covertly, Seeker had watched Bilrog, trying to read the creature's expressions. Obviously the Furmorian had tangled with something that had nearly killed it. Was it still so confident? Did it still think it could fight a war with the whole planet? Seeker's own lack of confidence drew it to Bilrog in hopes of finding its concerns echoed by another. And perhaps in the hope that the other had the answers it lacked.

Finally, the ursoid could contain itself no longer and blurted out, "Bilrog, why in the world did you come here?"

Bilrog raised its head and stared truculently at Seeker for several moments. Finally, the warrior sighed. "Why did I come here? Do you think it is because I want to be a Questioner, to go from world to world listening to problems and trying to find solutions? Is that what you think?

"Well, you'd be wrong if that was what you thought. I am here for one reason and one reason only. To bring glory to my people. We are the mightiest race in the universe. We have fought many wars all across the galaxy, battling for the Emperor. Yes. We are a mighty people."

Bilrog sat back to ease the pain of its wounds. It glared around at the others, particularly at the sneering face of Longarm. Finally, it began to speak again. "A mighty people. Yes. Our planet is much larger than this one. The gravity is very great. We are, as a result, very strong.

"Our world is a savage one, filled with dangerous animals. Our rise to lordship of our planet was a long and bloody trail. And then the Emperor came and offered us a chance for glory in his service. We became his Elite Guard. We traveled the galaxy in mighty warships and crushed world after world. None could stand against us.

"But there are more worlds than there are Furmorians. And though ten of us could destroy hundreds of any other race, the Empire began to falter. And finally, it fell, pulled down by its own weight and by the distance between the stars."

Bilrog fell silent and gazed off into the distance, as if measuring the galaxy with its mind. "Yes," the warrior finally said in a musing tone, "the Empire fell and we were scattered across the face of the galaxy. Some never found their way back to Furmoria. But some did, and they brought the warrior ways with them. We have kept those ways alive ever since.

"Now we fight wherever there are wars. We are soldiers of fortune, hunters, the most able killers in the galaxy. There is no creature, no game, too powerful for us. There is nothing we haven't killed."

"Except a whole planet," Seeker said softly.

Bilrog nodded. "Yes. This is the mightiest enemy in the

galaxy. Imagine! A whole planet that seeks to kill the sentient life that lands on its surface! The power and resources of a whole world aimed against any who would dare challenge it! What an opportunity for glory! If Bilrog conquers it, the name of Bilrog will echo in the halls of the Furmorians forever!"

Longarm laughed. "Echo is right! Now tell them the truth, Bilrog. Or do you want me to?"

Bilrog glared at the Teacher. "Truth? What do you mean, truth? I've told the truth."

"Partially at best," Longarm replied. "Huh. When the Empire fell, Furmoria's neighbors fell on Furmoria and burned the planet bare. No one came back to re-establish the old ways and carry on the traditions of the warrior clans, Bilrog. Furmoria is a dead world, killed by the hatred of those crushed by its lords.

"And the Furmorians themselves? Ah, yes, the mighty warriors! The ones who wander so picturesquely all across the galaxy to fight and hunt and kill for sheer glory? Hah! The truth is they are little better than bragging beggars, ne'er-do-wells who scrounge for any kind of work from one world to the next. Glory? Hah! They'll kill for a crust of bread! And Bilrog claims it comes for the glory of the Furmorians! Hah! Ask it how many of its people still exist. How many, eh, warrior? Shall I tell them? What is it, ten, fifteen?"

"One," Bilrog said softly. "One. I am the last."

Seeker looked confused, turning from Longarm to Bilrog and back. "But . . . but . . . if that's true . . . then why are you here, Bilrog?"

The Furmorian sat in stony silence, its eyes fixed on Longarm with glaring intensity. "Shall I answer that one, too, Bilrog?" the Teacher asked gently. Bilrog nodded slightly.

Longarm looked around the group with a grin. "Bilrog comes to Labyrinth for perhaps the most sensible reason of all. Yes, undoubtedly the most sensible.

"Bilrog comes here to fight a last, impossible battle. Bilrog comes here to die, like a warrior."

VIII.

They sat silently for a long time. Finally, Seeker raised its eyes to the grinning face of Longarm and asked softly, "Do you know why each of us is here, Teacher?"

The smile disappeared from Longarm's face and the Teacher nodded slowly. "Know? Yes, I know. And the reason is not always as it seems. Indeed, it may not even be what you yourself think it is. There is much that is uncertain, and it would be a rare creature indeed that could see into the future and tell precisely how its actions will turn out and what their impact will be. And yet, to decide on a course of action implies that you know where that course will take you."

"Surely we know the general direction," Bilrog protested.

"Do you?" Longarm sneered. "You come here to die with glory. What if you survive and actually find Sanctuary? Heh? What then? Do you become a Questioner? Do you wander throughout the galaxy helping others, you who come from a race that once spread fear and hatred and destruction far and wide?

"No. I tell you, you all have many reasons to be here. Some you tell to others to justify yourself in their eyes. Others you tell to yourself to justify yourself in your own eyes. Others you cannot even speak of."

Longarm gazed around at them all with an ironic glance. "You, Seeker, once said you knew why H*mb*1 was here because it told you. Hah! Told you! I imagine it spun a pretty tale, one of a planetwide plague that nearly wiped out its species. A plague that left only a few alive, and those dedicated to living in harmony with nature, dancing the dance of life with the planet as their partner. Ha! And that it had come here to dance that dance in the most terrible of all places, a virtual holy dance! Heh? Am I right?"

Seeker stared at the Teacher in confusion. Its eyes drifted to H*mb*1, who lay quite still, not yet fully recovered from the poison the spider had injected into its system. "Uh, yes, I mean, that's sort of what H*mb*1 told me . . ."

Longarm laughed out loud. "And I imagine you saw

H*mb*1 as one of the survivors of that plague? One of those who had lived through it and learned the dance? Heh?"

The ursoid nodded silently, Longarm's words disturbing it deeply. What was the Teacher driving at? "You mean . . . are you saying there was no plague?"

"Oh, no. There was a plague. And quite a lethal one at that. But it took place over three thousand years ago! And it was solved with help from the scientists of the First Empire. The famous dance H*mb*1 tells of was created several hundred years later, by a bunch of religious fanatics who took control of the culture and wanted to keep their race at a very primitive level. With themselves in charge, of course. They were defeated in a rather vicious civil war. Now they are a mere handful, a small minority religious group on a planet of teeming billions. They are slowly dying out.

"H*mb*1 was sent here by their leader in hopes of discovering something that might be used to revive their dying faith. If the dance, which lies at the core of their beliefs, can be revitalized, then there is hope. On their own world it is useless at present, for the whole planet is one vast city and nature is utterly subjugated and virtually invisible."

Seeker looked over at H*mb*1. "Is that all true?" the ursoid asked, its voice anxious and confused.

H*mb*1 buzzed softly. "Yes. It is all true. So far as it goes. Longarm indicated that the Holy One sent me. This is true. But I volunteered for the mission. I wanted to come. I wanted to dance Labyrinth. Ever since I first heard of this place, I have wanted to come here and dance. The Teacher is correct that nature is dead on my world. We have killed it utterly, far more effectively than our ancestors did before the First Plague. I am here to revive the Dance of Life. For it will be needed in the future. The plague is bound to come again, for we have sinned even more gravely than the first time. When it comes we must be ready. For only through the Dance of Life will our race be able to survive."

Longarm hooted. "Survive, yes, with you and yours as its rulers! And what makes you think the plague will return, eh? Will it come because it came before? Pretty poor logic, that. Or will it come for another reason?" The Teacher leaned forward, suddenly intent, its eyes narrowed, its gaze sharp and piercing. "Eh? Will it come for another reason? Will it come because someone goes to the most deadly planet in the galaxy and finds a deadly plague and brings it back? Eh?"

For long moments, they were all silent, staring with surprise from H*mb*1 to Longarm and back again. Then H*mb*1 buzzed softly and spoke in a bare whisper. "How do you know these things?"

Longarm chuckled deep in its throat. "Come, I have my secrets, too!"

"And a damned fine spy network, it seems to me!" Bilrog muttered, its voice edged with anger.

The Teacher chuckled again and turned to Thisunit. "And would you care to tell us why you have come to Labyrinth?"

Thisunit sat and stared back at Longarm. "Perhaps you should tell this unit's story for it. It appears to this unit that you probably know it well. And then if you tell it, it will take on a greater air of validity."

The Teacher nodded. "An interesting idea. I accept. I will tell your tale as though I were you. When I am done, you may comment if you like and correct any mistakes I make. Does that seem satisfactory to everyone?"

They all mumbled their assent as Longarm swept its eyes from one to another. Satisfied with their agreement to its proposal, the Teacher hunched itself down and pulled its long arms into the sleeves of its robe. Its face went blank and masklike in imitation of Thisunit. They were all astounded at the transformation. The Teacher actually managed to look like the other creature!

IX.

"Beneath this robe, this unit is vastly different from what most of you would suspect. This unit is part of a species which is a group entity. We have no individual identity as other species know it. Indeed, we have no separate physical identity at all on our home planet. We are all literally merely units in an overall matrix.

"When we must leave our planet for some reason, we place the individual unit into a bio-mechanical framework engineered for the specific task to be accomplished. For example, this unit is an information-gathering construct with many

extensions specifically designed to gather data and take sam-
ples. This unit's visual and auditory sensors can reach far into
the ranges of waves generally beyond that available to most
biological species. This unit can see far into the infrared and
can obtain detailed internal analyses of your structures because
its vision extends equally far into the very, very short wave-
lengths.

"But the largest portion of this unit's structure is taken up by
a very high-level computer, capable of storing trillions upon
trillions of bits of information and processing them at the speed
of light.

"Why was this unit sent here to Labyrinth? Quite obviously
to gather information, to accumulate data, to extrapolate that
data into patterns and to construct models based on those
patterns. That is the sole function of this unit."

Longarm suddenly turned back into itself and leered at
Thisunit. "How am I doing so far?"

Thisunit paused for an instant before responding. "Everything you have said correlates very closely with what this unit
would have stated on its own."

The Teacher grinned. "Good. I thought it might. Ah, but all
this is just window-dressing, isn't it? For we still haven't asked
the real question, have we?" They all looked at the Teacher
with confusion on their faces. "Surely, you can figure it out?
No? You surprise me. And the whole miserable lot of you
claim to come from sentient species! Just shows how far
sentience has fallen in today's galaxy! Well, then, the obvious
question is *why* did the overmind of which Thisunit is just a
tiny piece send it to Labyrinth to collect data in the first place?
What earthly, or unearthly, good could the collection of such
data do? What could the overmind use it for? Eh? I think we
should let Thisunit answer that question." Longarm sat back
and stared fixedly at Thisunit.

The robed and cowled figure sat without moving or speaking
for a few moments. "This information was never meant to be
revealed. This unit has no instructions in its program which
allow for the disclosure of this information. This unit cannot
respond."

Longarm laughed out loud. "True, only too true. You see,
friends, Thisunit is really just a program, a tiny, limited piece
of the overmind with a tiny, limited knowledge of what it is

doing and why. A spectrograph doesn't know why it gathers in light waves and breaks them apart. A thermometer doesn't know why it goes up and down when the temperature changes. And Thisunit doesn't really know why it collects data. Oh, it knows its mission here well enough. When it has gathered enough information to allow it to construct an all-encompassing model for what is happening here on Labyrinth, it will explode, and the explosion will provide the energy necessary to send a message across the galaxy to its home world, a message containing what it has learned. But it doesn't really understand why it is doing all this. Eh?"

"The Teacher is incorrect. This unit knows why it gathers data. The reason for its mission is very clear. That is why this unit has such utter dedication to what it is doing. This unit understands precisely what it is doing and why." Thisunit paused slightly. "It is just that this unit cannot tell others of its mission."

"Ah." The Teacher nodded. "I understand. Then shall we go back to our previous method? Shall I be Thisunit again and tell the others?"

Thisunit shrugged slightly. "If it suits you. This unit senses that it has no choice in this matter and that you will reveal its mission whether it wishes you to or not."

"True," Longarm sighed dramatically, "only too true. Well, then, to my task." And as before, the Teacher transformed itself into a very good copy of the robed alien.

"The data which this unit gathers here on Labyrinth will be integrated into the most noble effort in the entire galaxy. The data, once it has been systematized and then transmitted, will become part of the data being gathered by the overmind to complete the System.

"The System! The summation of all knowledge! Imagine every piece of data in the galaxy integrated into one mass, one whole, with nothing left out, nothing out of place! The total galaxy, totally explained! This is the vast and holy enterprise the overmind has embarked on, the enterprise it has dedicated the last two millennia to. The System nears completion, the gaps in it are almost closed. Success is almost achieved.

"But one great anomaly exists. Labyrinth. It does not fit within the System as it currently exists. There is no way to understand or explain its sentience. The overmind knows nothing of it and can find nothing out. It is necessary to send units to Labyrinth to gather data and transmit it home. The gaps in knowledge must be filled. The System must be completed!"

Longarm slumped back into its own natural slouch once more and grinned at them all. "So that's why Thisunit is here. Its race is fanatically consumed by one idea, to complete its beloved System, to close the gap created by the mystery of Labyrinth." An ironic grin twisted the lips of the Teacher. "How many have come here to Labyrinth on this mission, Thisunit? How many have come and failed? Eh? Can you at least tell the others that?"

Thisunit nodded slightly. "Yes. This unit can reveal that information. This unit is the four hundred fifty-seventh unit sent to Labyrinth."

Bilrog sputtered with a mixture of surprise and hilarity. "Four hundred fifty-seventh? Ha! What happened to the others?"

"The previous units all failed."

The Furmorian laughed outright. "I told you logic would do no good here in this place! Only a strong right, and left, arm are any good on Labyrinth. Only . . ."

Longarm brayed aloud. "Strength! Logic! Cowardice! Dancing! Fools, the lot of you! There is no answer to Labyrinth, no way to approach it, no way to conquer it. At least not by methods any of you understand yet. Perhaps you, Seeker, come closer than any, for you, at least, are learning despair.

"No. You all have much to learn. Very much. The trouble with all of you is that Labyrinth keeps teaching, and you keep ignoring. Darkhider goes out and skulks around, running and hiding from everything. It survives and says 'Aha! The Slime Gods were right after all! Cowardice is best! I've made it this far because of my cowardice. All I have to do now is perfect my cowardice, and then I'll be sure to make it to Sanctuary!' Idiocy! Everything you experience you put in little boxes of your own making. Bilrog sees everything that happens to it in terms of bravery. Thisunit changes everything into logic. Ha!"

Longarm turned and gestured toward the still recumbent H*mb*1. "Ah, yes, and H*mb*1 here dances and tries to transform the whole world into a dance. But as our big buzzer just discovered, not all things on Labyrinth dance to its tune.

Ah, no, for its dance is that of a master species ordering all those weaker than itself. It is indeed a Dance of Life, but of the life of the dominant creatures that rule a planet. Here on Labyrinth one must dance as an equal, or better yet, as a subordinate to the planet itself, for here Labyrinth is the dominant one!

"And you, Seeker, what is it you change everything into? Eh? Not too sure, are you? Well, you'd better figure it out! That is, if you want to live much longer!" Longarm hooted long laughter and then, without another word or a backward glance, turned and shuffled into its own quarters.

X.

Thisunit checked the sap that dripped from the tree a second time to make sure. Poisonous. But only the day before it had been safe! Reluctantly, Thisunit transferred the data to the system it had created. And watched all the variables shift just slightly. Suddenly there were gaps where none had existed before.

How could such a thing be possible? Perhaps it was just that the system needed to be revised drastically, that the model Thisunit had constructed was faulty and needed to be replaced with a new one. Yes, that had to be the answer.

But what if the new model still doesn't work? Thisunit wondered. What if the collected data continue to refuse to fit neatly together? Then this unit will simply have to construct another system and then another and another until one finally works.

And if none of them works? But one *has* to! The universe is a logical place, based on laws and rules that can be discovered and understood. It has to be, or else what is the purpose to intelligence? A universe that isn't structured on logical principles would have no place for intelligence, no need for it. Sentience would be a mere fluke, an essentially useless thing that happened by mere chance.

But that could not be the case! Sentience is found everywhere in the galaxy. Next to arachnids, it is one of the most pervasive phenomena in the universe. And what is more, the universe *is* inherently understandable. Rules can be formulated. Systems can be set up.

And yet a nagging doubt was growing in Thisunit's mind. Systems could be set up. Limited systems. Systems that dealt with limited portions of reality. Systems that might well be closed on themselves, but which always remained open with respect to the rest of the universe.

What about *the* System? Was it just possible that small systems could be more or less closed, but that the larger a system became, the less chance there was to close it? And what then of a system that hoped to enclose the entire galaxy?

Another thought struck Thisunit, one that rocked it back and stunned it. Even if the entire galaxy could be explained, even if every single phenomenon could be fit neatly into its little niche in the total model, did it really mean anything? For after all, just because this galaxy fit the model perfectly didn't mean every galaxy would. There might be one little piece of information that lay somewhere in the universe, that lay there waiting, to shred the fabric of even the most complete and perfect system.

It would always be that way. There could always be one more fact, one more piece of information, one piece that could turn all the others upside down.

There was a paradox here, one that simply didn't compute. The kind of data Thisunit sought was the only sure knowledge, for it was the only kind that could be measured, checked, corroborated. And yet by its very nature, it was ultimately unsure because the measurements, the checkings, the corroborations were always subject to revisions. The data could approach certainty, but never, never reach it. And if certainty could never be reached, then the System could never be completed. And if the System could never be completed . . .

Thisunit was overwhelmed. Slowly it turned and began to retrace its steps to Start. These ideas had to be carefully sifted through, and the face of this hostile planet was hardly the place to do it. Thisunit needed time to concentrate, time to sort things out. Time to try and understand.

As it returned to safety, it wondered if the units that had preceded it had all come to the same conclusion. And if that was why all of them had detonated and sent back the same message . . . a simple, inarticulate scream of despair.

XI.

Bilrog felt something it had never felt before. Fear. It knew it was being stalked by some creature, some creature that was stronger and more deadly than anything it had met before on Labyrinth. Something it might not be able to handle.

The warrior shook its head as if trying to dislodge the fear. After all, it told itself, I am the mightiest killer in the universe. I have fought in wars all across the galaxy. I have . . .

You are afraid, the small voice deep inside it said softly. Afraid for the first time in your life.

NO! Bilrog denied. Not afraid. Apprehensive perhaps. But . . .

What, after all, is bravery? the voice asked. Isn't it simply the willingness to face the things that are too fearful for most to face?

Yes, Bilrog agreed slowly, that sounds right.

So the key lies, then, perhaps, in what fearful means. Would you say fearful describes things that are bad for us?

Certainly, Bilrog agreed, but not all things that are bad for us are fearful. A thorn in the foot, or a piece of rotten meat, those are bad for us, but no one would call them fearful.

Good, the voice responded. Then the fearful must be that which is bad for us in a major way, a life-threatening way?

Yes, Bilrog answered.

But how do you know that something is bad for you in that way?

Well, Bilrog replied thoughtfully, you just know. Or in some cases you learn, either because others tell you, or you see what happens to them, or you experience it yourself.

So, knowledge is involved.

Of course, Bilrog nodded silently. Knowledge is involved with bravery. The Furmorian looked nervously over its shoulders, trying to catch a glimpse of the thing that was on its trail. If only I can make it back to Start in time, before it attacks, I may have a chance, the warrior told itself.

The voice returned. Would you call a warrior brave if it went to meet a foe it knew it could not defeat? Or if it went unprepared? Or unnecessarily? Assuming, of course, that it had a choice.

Bilrog snorted. Of course not. I'd call that kind of warrior a rash warrior, not a brave warrior.

So then there is a difference between rashness and bravery?

Yes, Bilrog replied.

Just as there is a difference between bravery and cowardice?

Of course, Bilrog answered. A cowardly warrior is like a rash warrior in a way. The cowardly warrior doesn't understand what is worst for it. It thinks that by avoiding the fight it is avoiding the bad. But in fact, it simply creates a different bad which actually is worse than what it was trying to avoid.

Ah, the voice said, so then bravery falls between two extremes, between rashness and cowardice.

Yes, Bilrog agreed, I suppose that is true.

And the major difference between it and the two extremes is that the brave warrior knows better what is bad for it and what is not? The brave warrior has superior knowledge of the bad?

That seems right.

Then is it brave to do something you know is bad for you? That is, as long as you aren't doing it to avoid something which is even worse?

I suppose not, Bilrog responded, slightly annoyed. Why did this foolish voice pop into its mind at times like this?

Because, the voice replied, it is at times like this when you most need it. If knowledge and bravery are so closely related, Bilrog, is what you are doing wise? And if not wise, then how can it be brave? Yet you seek to be brave. You claim it is the major force that drives you onward. You want to show the whole galaxy how brave the last of the Furmorians is. But is that really what you are showing them? Or are you being unwise and hence unbrave? Are you in reality being foolish and either rash or cowardly?

Bilrog stopped, its mind suddenly awhirl with new ideas. It turned around and looked back on its own trail, back down the way it had come for the last hour or so, stalked by some creature it knew would be its death. The thing that followed was huge and strong beyond anything the warrior had ever fought. Huge and strong, but slow. And here I am, Bilrog admitted, walking slowly over territory I know quite well, walking slowly while it comes closer and closer.

And why am I walking so slowly? Because I believe it is cowardly to run from an enemy. Even an enemy I know can kill me. Because I believe it is brave to fight against any odds even when the fight isn't necessary. I'm not protecting any cubs. There are no cubs. I'm not protecting my mate. There are no mates. I am simply living by a code which I have accepted as being certain knowledge. But if the knowledge that leads to bravery is a true understanding of that which is truly bad for one, then the knowledge I have lived by for so long is false knowledge. And what I have called bravery is really either rashness or cowardice!

Bilrog turned toward Start and began, for the first time in its life, to run from an enemy, an enemy it knew was slower and would never be able to catch it. As it ran, the warrior silently said, thank you.

You're welcome, came the reply.

XII.

H*mb*1 was dancing poorly. Twice now it had almost lost the rhythm and caused the danger it sought to avoid to come closer.

Longarm is right, it thought. There is something subtly wrong with my dancing. What can it be? Most of the time it works. Why did it fail with the spider?

The dancer stood still and thought. Longarm's words came back to it. Is the Teacher right when it says I dance the dance of a superior trying to control subordinates? I have always thought of it as a Dance of Life. But isn't the issue really whose life I am dancing? If I am merely dancing my life, or that of my species, then the Teacher is right and it is no wonder the spider did not respond. Of course, some creatures would respond. They would be weaker than I am and would fall under my rhythms, become part of my dance. But stronger creatures, like the spider, would not. And how would Labyrinth respond?

There was another question, too. Perhaps even more important, perhaps even the key to the first one. Why am I here? The teacher is right in some ways, wrong in others. Someone had to come, but that someone didn't have to be me. I volunteered for this assignment while the others hung back. My reasons for coming are bound up with those of the Master Dancer, but are not identical by any means.

Why, then, did I come? To prove something to myself and to the others? To prove that I am the greatest dancer of all time, greater even than the Master Dancer? Greater even than those of long ago who danced their way out of the plague?

Did they really dance out of the plague? Or was it truly the way Longarm tells it, that the scientists found a serum that cured my people of the sickness? If that is the case, then what does it mean for the Dance?

Nothing. It means nothing, for the Dance is still valid, still true, no matter how it came to be. The facts don't matter in the case of the Dance. It is not something to be understood. It is something to be done. And the doing of it reveals its truth in a way no accumulation of historical fact could.

So the issue is still why I am here, why I volunteered instead of letting someone else come. H*mb*1 twirled about slowly, moving slightly even while deep in thought. The creature looked like nothing so much as a natural thing, a tree, a strange growth, blown gently by the wind. It was almost hard to notice the dancer, so well did it merge with the natural background around it.

Yes, it thought, doing the Dance proves its truth, so the Dance itself cannot be wrong. Then the question must come from somewhere else. Yes. It must come from the reason why one is doing the Dance.

Which comes back to why I am here on Labyrinth, here doing the Dance on this alien world. If I am indeed here to prove something, even if it is that I am the best dancer, how does that affect my doing of the Dance?

Ah, can the Dance be done for a purpose? A purpose, that is, outside of the Dance itself? For isn't the Dance an end in itself? Isn't it to be done for no other reason than for the doing of it? Surely that must be the case.

Then what happens when it is done for a reason other than the sheer doing of it? For example, what happens when it is danced for the purpose of avoiding a plague? Or to find Sanctuary? Or to prove that the one doing it is the best dancer?

Then, H*mb*1 realized suddenly, it is no longer *the* Dance! It is merely *a* dance, one of many.

So how then, should *the* Dance be danced? Without purpose,

without intention, without any reason other than the mere doing of it. It must be danced for its own sake alone. It cannot be danced to avoid a dangerous creature or to get past a spider. For then it merely becomes a dance, one that may be wrong. If it is danced solely to be dancing it, then the spider will not even be a factor. Nothing will matter, nothing will even be noticed. The dancer will be totally enclosed in, totally consumed by, the Dance. The dancer will become the Dance.

Which meant that one had to totally give oneself up to the Dance. Motivation, intention, all had to go. There must be infinite resignation, infinite letting go of all hope, of every aspect of self, desire, purpose.

Can I do that? H*mb*1 wondered. Can I let go that completely? And if I do, then will that get me across the face of Labyrinth to Sanctuary? And if the answer is no, then why am I doing the Dance on this planet in the first place? For then I could just as well have stayed home!

There was a paradox here. To do the Dance well enough to get across the face of Labyrinth, one had to give up wanting to get across the face of Labyrinth! Not just a little bit of giving up, but totally, utterly, completely, infinitely. Only by no longer being interested in getting to Sanctuary could one dance one's way there! It made no sense. H*mb*1 had come here to dance its way to Sanctuary. But it couldn't do that if it in any way wanted to do it. Wanting it made it impossible. Only not wanting it made it possible to get it! But then why do it?

H*mb*1's mind went round and round the paradox, trying to find a way past it. There was no way. It wasn't a question of something unlikely, or difficult, or doubtful. This was something utterly impossible! The dancer tried to think it through and couldn't. Perhaps, it thought, I would have the strength to give up on my own intentions, to infinitely resign myself. That move I might be able to make. But the next move!!?? To get exactly what I had originally wanted and given up by the very act of giving it up? That move I cannot even comprehend. It makes my head hurt to even think of it. For if I give up what I want with the intention of getting it back by giving it up, I haven't really, infinitely given it up! And therefore the Dance will do me no good. And the next spider will kill me for sure. Only if I . . .

H*mb*1's mind came to a grinding halt. I cannot think these

things, it admitted. I must go back to Start. If I stand here and think, surely something will come along sooner or later, something that can see through the dance I weave, and it will kill me.

Slowly, reluctantly, H*mb*1 turned and headed back toward Start. Will I be able to solve this paradox once I am there? it wondered. Can it be solved? Or is my dancing doomed and am I the meal of a spider?

XIII.

There is a problem. Oh, yes, a problem. Darkhider dug furiously. The thing behind it dug even more swiftly.

It was a thing very unlike all the others Darkhider had seen before. Long, narrow, saurian. It was fast, had sharp teeth, and big front feet that were perfect for digging. It was a thing of nightmares, a thing that somehow had managed to circumvent the great Law of Compensation. But then, that was to be expected, for it had never been created by the Slime Gods at all. No. It was a creature of Labyrinth.

Darkhider had been slinking, hiding, dashing from cover to cover, shivering in fearful ecstasy. It saw a huge, furry monster with many teeth and sharp claws. But the creature was slow, and Darkhider scampered out of its way. Besides, it seemed to be intently stalking other game. Darkhider idly wondered if it was after one of the other Pretenders. If so, there might well be one less of them by nightfall. So much the better, the saurian decided. That would simply make things easier.

It had been worried when Longarm had been exposing them one by one, telling their real reasons for coming to Labyrinth. If the Teacher knew of Darkhider's mission, would it seek to thwart it? Surely it would. So the saurian had crouched in shivering fear the whole time the simian had spoken, waiting hopelessly to hear the words which would expose it.

But wonder of wonders, Longarm had never gotten to Darkhider! It had told the secrets of Bilrog, Thisunit, and H*mb*1, but had left off speaking before getting to Darkhider! Did that mean that it did not know? Darkhider prayed to the Slime Gods that that was indeed the case!

The next day, today, it had gone out, filled with cautious

optimism. Its mission would succeed! It would find Sanctuary, then return in its Questioner ship to its own planet and lead the return to Labyrinth! It would . . .

And that had been its undoing. It had been thinking and not fearing, hoping instead of cringing, and the thing that was digging after it had appeared from nowhere.

It had already bitten a good chunk out of Darkhider's tail. The pain kept surging up and almost overwhelming the saurian. But Darkhider kept digging furiously.

Its claws scraped against rock. It twisted up and scrabbled wildly. Rock again. Downward. Rock again. With a hiss of despair it sank down to the floor of the tunnel it had dug. Behind it could hear the sound of digging and snuffling. The thing was almost on it. The end was almost there. Soon Darkhider would be in the belly of the beast that hunted it. There was no hope.

Futilely it patted its harness again and again, hoping that somehow a miracle would occur and the fetishes would reappear. They had all been lost when the beast had caught Darkhider the first time, the time the chunk had been bitten from the saurian's tail. They had struggled and the creature's claws had ripped the talismans right off the harness. Darkhider had twisted wildly then and managed to wrest free. It had fled with a fear deeper than any it had ever known.

Now it was all over. The thing would be there in a few moments. With its claws and its teeth and its hunger. Darkhider was no match for it. It would rend the saurian to pieces and then swallow those pieces. There was no hope, no way out.

The thing hissed in anticipation. Darkhider looked up and saw it. Saw its ugly, tooth-filled snout. Smelled its foul breath. Death. This was death. Everything had been in vain.

Suddenly a great anger filled Darkhider. An almost mindless fury flooded the saurian's thoughts, driving eons of habit and belief down beneath its overpowering force. Everything turned upside down, everything blurred and then took on a new focus. Nothing mattered anymore. All plans, all schemes, all thoughts vanished. Only one thing mattered.

With a hiss of infinite rage, Darkhider launched itself forward in attack.

XIV.

It was tall, narrow, and appeared to be made of crystal lumps piled loosely on top of each other. Tall: about six and a half feet. Narrow: perhaps six inches through the middle. Crystal: not really rocks, but some substance, warm to the touch, that looked like crystal and was translucent like crystal.

Seeker stood and stared at the thing in wonder. What in the world could it be? Somehow the Pretender was certain the tall crystal thing was both alive and not of this planet. For an instant a wild idea flashed across its mind. Could it be a Pretender, too? Seeker laughed at itself. A crystal?

The ursoid reached out gingerly and placed its paw on the surface again. Yes, definitely warm to the touch. No sense of menace at all. Seeker idly tried to lift it to see how heavy it was. Surprisingly light. One could easily carry it for a short distance.

Why not? Seeker grasped it firmly and lifted, then rested the tall crystal thing against its shoulder. Where to carry it? That way looked good, back the way Seeker had just come. The ursoid began to retrace its steps. How far should it be moved? Hmmmmm. Over there seemed right.

Seeker put the thing down and stepped back. Yes, that seemed to be a good place. Yes, it belonged there, felt right there.

Fear welled up in the Pretender. What had it been doing? Picking something up and carrying it? Some strange thing, some creature? Here on Labyrinth? What if it had been poisonous? What if it was part of some elaborate trap, some trick the planet played on the unwary? What if . . . Panic rose up in the ursoid and with a whine of terror, it fled, leaving the six-foot tower of crystal behind.

XV.

"Still there, huh?" Longarm said when Seeker told it what had happened. "Huh. Getting closer. Wonder if it will ever make it."

"What . . . what are you talking about? Do you know what that thing is?"

"Of course. It's the same thing you are. A Pretender."

"That crystal thing is a Pretender?" Seeker was dazed with amazement.

Longarm nodded. "Yep. Came here maybe two, three hundred years ago. Left Start almost immediately. Been out there ever since, moving slowly, slowly toward Sanctuary."

Seeker just gaped. Finally the ursoid said, "That thing moves? It's on its way to Sanctuary? How . . ."

"You just found out how. It calls a creature to it, one capable of moving it. Then it talks the creature into moving it in the direction and the distance it wants to go. Stays there for a while, maybe ten, fifteen years, just getting used to the area, feeling safe there, making its peace with Labyrinth. Then another creature comes along and it gets moved again."

"But . . . but . . ." Seeker sputtered in confusion. "After I moved it I suddenly felt very afraid and I fled . . ."

Longarm nodded wisely. "Always the same. Doesn't want you hanging around. Never knows for sure what you might do to it. So it scares you. Sends you off packing. Next time you go out that way, I'd give it a wide berth. It has your wavelength, or whatever it operates on. No telling what it might do. Just steer clear of it and you'll be O.K. Range is pretty short."

The ursoid sat heavily on a rock, its head hanging. Longarm looked down at it and smiled slightly, then sat down next to it. For many moments the two of them sat there, wrapped in deep mutual silence. When Seeker finally raised its eyes, they were filled with sadness and distress. "I . . . I don't think I'm going to make it, Teacher. I can't understand this place. It's just too much, too many things, too confusing. I . . . I don't know what I'm looking for, nor where to look, nor what it would look like. I just wander around on a planet that's trying to kill me and . . ." The ursoid ran out of words and dropped its eyes to the ground again.

Longarm laced its fingers together around its knees and said to Seeker, "Watch." The ursoid looked up and the Teacher rolled backwards off the rock, then up onto the top of its head. It balanced there for a second, then put its hands down to the ground and pushed off, springing upside down into the air. As it came down, it landed on one palm and again balanced perfectly. With a final shove off, it twisted and landed on its feet.

"Do that," Longarm commanded.

Seeker just stared. "I . . . I can't do that. I'm not built for it. You have long arms and . . ."

Longarm hooted a laugh. "Right. And I've been practicing it for years. The move is easy for me. Impossible for you. But there are moves that you could make which I couldn't. Physical moves, mental moves. Heh? I've never known what it's like to be swift and fly across the plains like the wind. Nor to feel the power of immense strength and razor-sharp claws.

"You, Seeker, you came here to find something, right? But it's something you've never seen and can't even describe."

"But . . . but I came here to become a Questioner."

"And what do you think that is?"

"You know what it is. You must know. You're a Teacher."

Longarm snorted and did a sudden backflip, landing on its hands once more. From that position, it spoke again. "A Teacher. This I could teach you more easily than what you are really asking for. You want me to teach you to be a Questioner, don't you, Seeker? You think it's something you can learn, like mathematics or geography, heh?"

"But if you're not here to teach us to be Questioners, why are you here?"

Longarm gestured to the horizon with one hand while maintaining its balance on the other. "There is your teacher. Labyrinth."

"A planet? A deadly planet? What can it teach me?"

"Fear. Humility. Hopefully wisdom." Longarm flipped upright. "If you're lucky, of course. Other virtues, too. Bravery. Generosity. Oh, all kinds of things."

"But couldn't you teach me those things?"

The Teacher shrugged. "Teach you to repeat formulas, yes. To do handsprings, possibly. Wisdom? Never. Seeker, if I taught you I would supplement your ideas, give you more knowledge, more understanding of things. But I wouldn't be able to change you. And that's what Labyrinth can do. It can change you."

"What do you mean, 'change' me?"

"I can describe fear, try to scare you with scary tales, all of those things. The Nurturers used to tell you tales when you were a cub, eh? Tales of what lay beyond the edge of the firelight, of the Weekroo, the one banished from the pack that lay in the dark waiting, waiting for a foolish cub to wander off. Heh. Good stories. Used to raise the fur along your back and make your crest stand up.

"But that isn't fear. Not real fear. That's just thinking about fear, reflection of fear. No. Real fear is when you see that death right there in front of you. When you feel the touch of the real Weekroo or the slimy embrace of a tentacle rising from the deep.

"No. I can't teach you fear. But Labyrinth can. Because Labyrinth is fear. And humility. And even wisdom."

"But why do I have to know these things?"

"Ha! You want to be a Questioner, don't you? Of course you do. You want it enough to die for it, which you very well may. Ha! So think about what a Questioner does. It goes to a planet that has put out a call for help, eh? And why would a planet put out a call for help? Because it is afraid! Very afraid. Utterly, totally afraid. And what help do you think a creature that did not understand and know fear to the very root of it would be on a planet like that?

"But fear isn't enough. There is so much more you must know."

"Then why aren't we being taught? Will we be taught in Sanctuary?"

Longarm laughed. "Always the curious one, eh, Seeker? No, you won't be taught anything in Sanctuary. If you don't learn all the lessons on the surface of Labyrinth, you'll never get to Sanctuary. And if you do, well, then, what is there to teach? No. Get to Sanctuary and the only thing they'll teach you is how to fly the ship that will take you out on your first mission as a Novice. And that's just a skill, not knowledge."

Seeker pondered for several moments. "You said Labyrinth would teach me wisdom."

The Teacher shook its head. "I said hopefully you would learn wisdom. Understand the difference between knowledge and wisdom and teaching and learning.

"Start with the easy one. There's no such thing as teaching. There's only learning. Teaching implies that somehow one creature can place knowledge, skill, whatever, in another. But that's not true. All a teacher does is make things available, to open things up, so to speak. The real work is learning. Learning is taking something into you and making it part of you. Hard work, that.

"That's a pretty quick and dirty explanation, but let's move on to the hard one. You can have knowledge of many things. How to do a handstand, how to chase down a springdasher, how to eviscerate a hornhead, how to fix a billigok nut so it isn't poisonous. You can even distinguish between several different kinds of knowledge, which we won't bother with here.

"But wisdom is different. It's not about a lot of things, but only about one thing. The most important thing of all."

"What's that?" Seeker said eagerly, leaning forward attentively.

Longarm howled with laughter and flipped into a one-hand handstand. "Not how to do a handstand, but why!" The Teacher came down onto both its feet and turned without another word. Seeker sat in speechless wonder and watched as the simian creature waddled back into its quarters.

XVI.

The other Pretenders came straggling back into Start in various states of disarray. Bilrog was quite out of breath from having run a long way. The huge Furmorian looked strangely sheepish and uncertain and went off to its quarters without joining the others for the evening meal.

Both H*mb*1 and Thisunit were so deeply preoccupied and sunk in thought, that neither one of the creatures so much as looked up or uttered a word while they ate.

But the most surprising of all was Darkhider. The little saurian had returned scratched, battered and bloody. Its harness and all the precious talismans were gone. Yet rather than slinking and whimpering, the creature strode along (with a pronounced limp) in a fashion markedly different from that which it had previously maintained. What was more, Darkhider was obviously bursting with impatience for someone, anyone, to listen to its tale.

Seeker nodded and smiled. The saurian scurried over to it,

almost stumbling over itself in excitement. Before the ursoid could even speak a greeting, Darkhider began. "There isss sssomething new, Ssseeker. Yesss. Sssomething hasss happened and there isss sssomething new."

"Explain," Seeker said, almost laughing outright at Darkhider's excitement.

"Yesss. Darkhider hasss dissscovered that there isss sssomething other than fear which Thinksss Before and Thinksss After gave to usss." The saurian drew itself up to its full height and looked Seeker in the eye. "A thing chasssed me. Yesss. A thing with many teeth and sssharp clawsss. I fled, fear giving me sssspeed like never before. Yet the thing wasss jussst asss fassst and took a big chunk out of my tail." Darkhider swished its tail around so that Seeker could see the gaping wound.

"But Darkhider had been clever, yesss, ssso clever. Darkhider had dug burrowsss for hiding. Ssso Darkhider dove into one of itsss holes and tried to hide, ssshaking with fear." The saurian trembled and hissed with remembered terror. "But the horrible creature, it digsss, oh, yesss, itsss big clawsss dig very well and it comesss digging after Darkhider. Ssso what can poor Darkhider do? Darkhider digsss deeper and deeper in fear. Oh, how frightened poor Darkhider isss!

"Then rock. Yesss, rock comesss then and Darkhider can dig no more. There isss no plassse to go, no plassse to cower in fear. And the terrible creature isss digging hard, coming clossser and clossser!"

Darkhider seemed to suddenly grow inches taller. "The thing isss about to grab poor Darkhider, to rend itsss flesssh, to sssspatter itsss blood, to eat it alive. And what can poor Darkhider, poor frightened, cowardly Darkhider do?" The saurian paused for dramatic effect. "Attack! Darkhider attacksss the dreadful creature. Darkhider fightsss it! Darkhider bitesss and sssscratches and hisssssses. And the thing isss frightened. It turnsss and runsss! Yesss! And Darkhider isss sssaved!"

The saurian fell quiet and gazed at Seeker, its eyes filled with self-wonder and amazement. "Thisss thing that Darkhider did, thisss thing, it isss courage, yesss?"

Seeker nodded. "Yes. It is courage. It came from your heart and it made you strong and unafraid."

"The creature, it wasss bigger and ssstronger than I wasss, yet it fled. Why?"

The ursoid laughed. "We have a saying on my planet, Darkhider. 'It's not the size of the cub in the fight, but the size of the fight in the cub.' It means that the one who wants to win the most probably will. You wanted to win, were suddenly sure you could. And you did. Besides, the thing wasn't expecting you to turn on it like that. You probably scared the wits out of it!"

Darkhider hissed with pleasure. "Yesss. It knew Darkhider wasss a runner, a hider. But when Darkhider turned and attacked . . . yesss, then it knew fear!"

Something Darkhider had said suddenly struck Seeker. "Darkhider," the ursoid asked softly, "you said it 'knew' you were a runner, a hider? How did it know?"

"All thingsss know we are runnersss and hidersss."

"All things on your planet. But how would something from this planet, something that had never been to your world, had never met a being of your species before, how would a creature like that 'know' what you were like?"

"It would . . ." Darkhider paused, looking confused. "It wasss like thingsss on my world. It wasss like sssomething from a nightmare, sssomething I have alwaysss dreaded."

"It came out of your own mind?"

Darkhider was thoughtful now. "Yesss. It could have come out of my mind. It wasss everything I have ever feared."

Seeker looked over at Thisunit and H*mb*1, then off in the direction Bilrog had gone. Finally, it gazed at the door of Longarm's quarters. "I wonder," the ursoid said softly, almost as if to itself, "if the things the rest met today were out of their own minds, if they were things they fear most."

Deep in thought, Seeker turned and began to walk up the hill toward its shack. If we all met the thing we fear the most today, it wondered silently, what was it I met and where did I meet it?

XVII.

Thisunit correlated the data and watched as the shifts occurred in the model. It shuddered slightly. The next step was the most critical one, the one that would decide if what Seeker was proposing was even possible.

Thisunit took the sample again. And then fed the reading into the model a second time. Once more it shifted, ever so slightly, opening new gaps.

It was true! Labyrinth was purposefully changing the inputs! The same berry sampled twice within a few moments gave different readings!

Thisunit moved back and began to think. It set all its warning sensors on full alert to warn it if anything potentially dangerous should appear in the vicinity.

Predictability. Suppose you told a sentient being that you had predicted it would do A. Then it could do just the opposite, B, and falsify your prediction.

Ah, but that was circular. If you told the being it would do A, then the telling had to be factored into the prediction. So you really should have predicted it would do B when you told it that it would do A. But that was circular, too. It could still go ahead and do A, in which case the prediction that it would do B was falsified.

But there was something much worse possible. If you told it it would do A in hopes that it would do B, it could always do C or D or E or anything at all. The system was not closed-ended. This was especially important because the more complex A was as an action, the more possibilities would open up.

Did that mean that the prediction itself, or the act of creating the prediction, changed the very thing being studied? Yes, that was clearly the case on the sub-atomic level.

What, then, did certainty mean? One plus one is two. Certainty. But the whole system was based on an assumption, on an uncertainty. Every system was. There was always a presupposition that could not be proven within the system itself.

The sun will rise in the east tomorrow. Certainty. But why? It could just as easily not come up. Just because it had come up every day in the past in the east was no certainty it would tomorrow. Even the fact that the planet turned from west to east didn't really guarantee certainty. There was an assumption there as well. Because the planet had always turned from west to east in the past didn't mean it always would. There was no logical contradiction in the idea that it would turn from east to west. In fact, Thisunit knew of planets that did.

Why did it seem so certain? Because it happened again and again, because we got used to it happening that way, got in the habit of it happening that way. But it was not necessary for it to happen in that way. It was not certain.

Longarm is a simian. Certainty. Yes, for the word 'Longarm' contained within it the meaning 'simian,' and all that sentence did was unpack the meaning of the word 'Longarm.' Simian was one of the defining characteristics of Longarm.

Longarm is a simian. Certainty. But did it matter? Was it important? Was certainty of that type worthwhile? Surely it was worthwhile, for it allowed a unit to investigate the full meanings of a word. And surprises were often discovered.

But they were all already there, obscured, but there. There was nothing truly new or revelatory involved. It was certainty, but it wasn't very important.

Is that the kind of certainty this unit searches for? No, it can't be. The System can't be that trivial. The System is trying to answer all the questions about the galaxy, to explain it right down to the last, tiny detail. And unless it is all contained in one word that can be unpacked for all its meanings, the kind of certainty this unit seeks is nothing like it.

Is there any other kind of certainty? Or is the only alternative nothing more than a constantly receding approximation? And if it is only such an endless process of approximation, can one accept such knowledge as final certainty for something truly important? Could it ever be used as the very basis of the System?

If objective certainty is a phantasm, a ghost of seeming substantiality that vanishes when a unit tries to grasp it, then either certainty must be a mere elusive dream, or it must reside in some other form of knowledge. If certainty, some kind, any kind, was not possible, then the whole System was a fraud. The very possibility that such a thing could be the case made Thisunit's mind reel with horror and despair. But if it wasn't the case, then what could that other form of knowledge that led to certainty be? What form would it take? What . . .

Thisunit felt itself falling, falling into an abyss, a horror of contradiction and uncertainty. It tried to save itself, tried to throw itself back up to the edge, tried to find wings to soar in the emptiness. But its mind was built to plod slowly and surely along the trail of objective certainty, a trail that dissolved utterly in the abyss. Flying required an inner certainty, a totally subjective state of mind. That state was called belief, and had nothing whatsoever to do with the rational and objective world Thisunit inhabited. Belief was only a word to the cowled being, a word that seemed to have no meaningful referents. Ironically, Thisunit's only hope lay in a state of mind it could not comprehend and which it would deny even existed.

The explosion flattened everything for fifty yards around. The energy from the explosion powered one last message from the transmitting unit. It was an inarticulate scream.

XVIII.

Four now. Just four. One gone. They had all heard the blast, all heard the message. It had rocked them all, knocked some over, knocked Darkhider unconscious.

It was hard to understand that Thisunit was dead. Dead. Not there any more. Memory. They missed the strange creature. For its death brought them each a little closer to its own.

Oddly enough, Bilrog seemed to be the most deeply affected. The Furmorian warrior had stayed in Start for several days after the death. Stayed and sat and stared and thought. When Seeker had approached Bilrog, the warrior had smiled wanly and said, "If so much intelligence can't win, what can?"

What had happened to Thisunit? None of them really knew. Longarm had muttered that the creature had strangled on its own knowledge, that its impossibly complex language had driven it insane and that it had committed suicide, that it had suffered from terrible indigestion and just blown up, that an explosive creature had attacked it and blown it up, that . . . The stories went on and on, each explanation more fantastic than the last. But Seeker could sense that even Longarm was disturbed by Thisunit's death.

Seeker had its own theory. What had happened to Thisunit was precisely the same thing that was happening to all of them. Labyrinth was feeding them precisely those things most likely to destroy them. The ursoid had asked Thisunit about this possibility just before it had gone out the last time. "Do you think the planet could be giving you purposefully confusing and contradictory data?" it had asked. Thisunit had received the idea with great agitation and anxiety.

But that would explain what was happening. Darkhider was sent the monster from its most horrible dreams, a monster meant to terrify and dismay it to the point where it could no longer function and would die. But Darkhider had found something inside itself, something it hadn't even expected was there. And Darkhider had beaten Labyrinth on that round.

Or was that what Labyrinth wanted? Was the planet testing them to find out not merely what they were but what they could become? Was the truth that Darkhider had passed and Thisunit had failed? If Thisunit had been fed data it could not correlate, was the purpose merely to destroy it or was it to try and force it to change, to find another way of dealing with the situation from within itself?

If that was true, what is Labyrinth trying to do to me? Seeker wondered. It gazed off across the plain it had come to on the other side of a small range of mountains. Not the same, no, but similar, filled with echoes and memories. Did Labyrinth know this? Had the planet guided Seeker to this particular place, this place that was so familiar?

Why? Labyrinth had shaken Darkhider from its fear. Labyrinth had taught Bilrog to run away. It had tried to force Thisunit to think in a different manner. What is it trying to teach me?

Seeker plodded across the plain. How different from the way it had once virtually flown. So swift, so sure. The fastest and the best. Only the most fleet of foot could escape the Chaser. Seeker's step became unexpectedly lighter with the memory.

And then power had come. Heaviness, yes, but immense power as well. And long claws. And a speed of a different sort. Such a strong Catcher! There had never been a stronger! And yet it hadn't been sheer strength that had made Seeker so good. No. It had been careful thought and reflection on the art of Catching. Reflection and practice. Only that combination had made the Catcher capable of catching things others would shun. Things like hornhead. Or crazyfangs. Yes. And even a poisontooth.

Seeker jogged along at a ponderous pace, its mind wrapped

in the past. It jogged to the east, toward where the sun rose. It went on and on, tireless, steady, absorbed with its thoughts.

And then it stopped. Its eyes followed the plain out and out. To where it rose up into the sky. Curved up and up and up until it was lost in the clouds.

Seeker gave a great cry of anguish and collapsed in a heap.

XIX.

H*mb*1 had finally found the thing it had been searching for. There off to the left.

Was this wrong? Perhaps in a way. It was self-conscious and there was at least some concern in H*mb*1's mind that the self-conscious aspect of it all put the dancer in grave danger.

At the same time, neither the dance nor the dancer was passive by nature. The key was the intention once in the dance, once doing it. Then self, the dancer, had to go away by blending into the dance. H*mb*1 knew that if it could not do that it was doomed anyway. It would never survive Labyrinth.

But to do this again? And to do it so soon? Then again, why not? Intention was the issue, not time. There were no new steps to be learned. All that was left to be learned was to let go of all steps, to learn how to forget.

The spider sensed the approach of the dancer and began to move itself toward its prey. H*mb*1 stood totally still, reaching out with its senses and its mind, trying to find the rhythms of the monster. They were strange, strange. Yet if one . . . let go . . . and then . . .

H*mb*1 began to move. The spider stopped, waiting. H*mb*1 moved closer and closer and the spider waited patiently.

Then a strange thing happened. H*mb*1 seemed to fade, to transform. Somehow the four legs appeared to be eight, the body changed shape, the motions became different, utterly other, totally un-H*mb*1-like. The spider tensed, then began to move as well, following the motions of the other, adding variations, shifts, nuances.

Together they danced and danced until the spider became weary and went back to its tree to rest.

H*mb*1 moved off across the face of the planet, dancing. And yet, there was no dancer, but only the dance.

XX.

The warrior crept to the top of the ridge and peered over. There were three of them in sight. Were there others hidden in the bushes or the rocks? Keen eyes swept the site. Nothing. Only the three.

Was three too many? Yes and no. The real question was whether or not it was necessary to fight. And the answer was yes, it was. They lay directly between the warrior and its goal. There was no way around. What was behind was worse. So it was straight ahead or not at all.

The warrior began to plan its attack. Both knives came out, one in each hand. Speed, accuracy, surprise. Attack from the left, letting the two on the right block each other. Kill one, then there would be only two. Now. Move.

Bilrog sprang over the ridgetop and leapt down the other side, running in great bounds. The warrior was on its first enemy before the creature even had time to react. It shrieked as the two knives slammed into it, killing it before it even hit the ground.

The other two threw themselves at Bilrog in a blind fury. The warrior sidestepped one and slashed it all down the length of its body. The other hit Bilrog square on the chest and they went down in a tangle. But the battle was swift. Both knives jabbed several times and the thing fell limp in death.

The third one was on its feet, stunned by its wound but still dangerous. Bilrog circled it. It lunged in despair and the warrior danced back out of its way. It stood its ground and glared at the Furmorian, its eyes shining with hatred.

Bilrog nodded and saluted it. Then one hand went up and flashed down in a swift arc. From it a flash of metal gleamed out as it flicked across the space separating the two combatants. The knife buried itself to the handle in the beast's throat. With a last glare of hatred, it slumped into death.

Cautiously, Bilrog approached, its knife ready, its senses fully alert in case of a trick. But the other was good and thoroughly dead. The Furmorian pulled out its knife and wiped it clean on the fur of its fallen foe.

Leaving the three where they lay, Bilrog walked to the top of the next ridge and gazed over at what lay beyond. Sanctuary lay somewhere in that direction; the warrior was sure of it. And if that was indeed true, then . . . The Furmorian hesitated to think the thought all the way through and laughed out loud instead. If it was indeed true, it continued, then what a joke on all of us!

XXI.

When Bilrog went over the ridgetop, Longarm came out from behind the boulder that had hidden it. The Teacher walked over to the dead creatures and touched them gently, wiping away the blood and sealing the wounds. After a few moments they stirred and finally stood. Longarm gestured to them and they ran off.

The Teacher stood and gazed in the direction Bilrog had taken. Would it be those two, then? Bilrog and H*mb*1? Seeker was unconscious, in a state of such shock it might never recover. Darkhider was almost dead of its wounds. The saurian had tried to be as brave as it had once been fearful. No moderation, that was the creature's problem, Longarm thought. That and a purpose that has no place here, a voice added in its mind. True, the Teacher nodded. True. But there was always a chance.

There is always a chance, the voice sounded, coming from nowhere and yet from everywhere. But the chance of success is always much smaller than the chance of failure. Because the ways of failing are infinite and the way of success is only one.

Longarm sighed. And yet I rather liked Seeker. Is there any hope for it?

Hope? Yes. Hope. The creature must come to terms with itself before it can come to terms with me. It has been pushed over the edge of sanity. Thisunit could not fly. We will see if Seeker has wings.

Aye. Well, I'll get back to H*mb*1 now.

Yes, the voice said. And Longarm disappeared.

When a spider hurls itself down from a fixed point . . . it always sees before it only an empty space wherein it can find no foothold however much it sprawls.

Soren Kierkegaard

⚜

I.

There were nine of them, three threes. All were old and grizzled, older than any Nurturers Strong had ever seen. And all nine of them had the same strange smell, a mélange of alien scents that the Catcher could not identify.

The nine sat around Strong in a circle to signify the pack and its unity. At first they asked the Catcher many questions, both about itself and about its battle with Crusharm. Eventually, as Strong had known they would, they brought up the issue of the plain.

"And so," a brown-hued one growled, "you left the pack and went off on your own to chase a creature that had no food value for the pack?"

Strong lifted its chin and stared directly at the Nurturer. "Yes, I did,. I had chased many creatures to the Catchers the day before. Enough for the pack to eat for several days. I did not shirk my duties to the pack."

A stooped, grey creature took over the questioning. "Of course, of course. It was a romp. Come, come, Walksteady, you did the same when you were young. We all did. That's why we have superior bloodlines. Heh, heh. The romp is not the issue here. The issue is what was seen during the romp. Tell us again, Catcher, what you think you saw."

"I saw," Strong replied, stressing the word slightly, "the plain rising into the sky. Off in the distance, it just went up and up, right into the clouds."

"But you couldn't have seen such a thing, since such a thing does not exist," scolded a reddish-colored member of the circle.

The grey one waved a paw in remonstrance. "Bah, Redfur, time is past for that nonsense. The Catcher knows what it saw. It's seen it several times, am I not right?"

Strong nodded solemnly, pleased that at last one of the Nurturers appeared to be taking what it said seriously. "Yes. I have returned to that place seven times. Each time the plain rises in the same manner."

"Never thought of going any closer, of investigating it up close?" When Strong looked a bit disconcerted, the grey Nurturer chuckled. "Ah, well, I imagine you would have sooner or later."

The grey one addressed the other members of the circle, saying, "Just shows that the experiment is only partly success-ful. I for one think it will never go beyond this."

"Nonsense," Redfur growled. "This is a particularly diffi-cult bloodline and you know it. Most of the others have responded quite nicely."

A honey-colored Nurturer snorted. "Huh. We don't need any more dullards. That's why this line is so important to us. We hoped to suppress the K factor without inhibiting initiative. Greyback is correct. Though I would not even give the experiment credit for partial success. It's a dismal failure. This Catcher was altered, by all that's holy! Altered and still the K factor was not overcome."

"On the contrary," added Greyback. "If anything, the altering strengthened the K factor by giving psychological motivations previously lacking in the subject. I agree, Swift-thought. My previous remark was meant as irony."

Redfur growled deeply, lips curling away from fangs. "Are you two suggesting that the Reserve should be closed and the experiment stopped? I know you, Greyback. You've always been opposed to this project. You fought it in the Council. But it is part of the Solution, and you know that the Solution cannot be altered . . ."

"Bah!" Greyback snarled. "That's the kind of rigid thinking

that made it necessary to call for help in the first place! Redfur, it's been seventeen generations since the Solution was instituted. Seventeen!"

"And do you really believe seventeen generations have changed our natures? Do you think we are so superior to our ancestors of the Time of Confusion that we can . . ."

"Again, bah! No, I don't think we are better than those at the Time of Confusion in any way but in our own knowledge of those times and how we got out of them! I do not believe for one instant that it was the intention of the Questioner to change the nature of our species by means of the Solution."

"Ah. And perhaps you will enlighten us as to what was the Questioner's intention?" The sneer in Redfur's voice was heavy.

Greyback sighed and winked at Strong. "You see, young one, even your elders are far from perfect." The Nurturer turned a patient eye to Redfur and spoke softly. "You've heard me say this many times in the Council, friend. But if you wish, I will say it again. The Solution was not meant to become a permanent state. It was merely a temporary measure to give us time to get back on our feet so that we might take our own measure and come to better understand who and what we are. It was not meant to change who and what we are, merely to allow us a modicum of intelligent species self-control."

Redfur waved a paw at the plain that surrounded them. "And all this, constructed at immense cost, was just a temporary measure?"

"Yes," Greyback nodded. "And no. It was an experiment to teach us how we came to be, on the assumption that that would help us understand what we are. There is no plain any longer, Redfur, no habitat similar to what we evolved in. We took care of that very thoroughly in the Time of Confusion. 'All this,' as you so eloquently phrase it, recreates what we destroyed in our confusion and gives us a place to raise a certain number of our own under conditions approximating those of a better time. It allows us to delve deeply into our own past, to that time when we became what we are. Hopefully, understanding will come from going back to our own roots.

"And besides that, the Reserve has produced some very fine Nurturers. I came from here. So did you. So did most of those on the Council.

"But most of us did not. Don't forget what the Questioner found. Skulkers in a ruin. A species gone mad. A sane remnant holding out and crying into the darkness for help. No, most of us came from the Shambles, were born and raised there."

Redfur waved a paw in protest. ".Your usual speech. As always, we disagree on fundamentals. The Questioner was quite specific. The Reserve was built to regenerate our species, to transform us into what we could be. We were a possibility gone wrong. The Solution was to make us an actuality. And the project here on the Reserve must continue until we are successful. This individual," Redfur went on, pointing to Strong, "is a failure. Its K factor is beyond tolerance limits. I wouldn't be surprised if its aggressive behavior was somehow tied to the excessive K factor. It must be removed from the Reserve before it causes too many side effects. This fight with another Catcher is just one example of the kind of thing that can happen. Who knows how that fight has affected the others in its pack?"

"High K factor, yes. But excellent bloodline, too. I do not agree that K factor is the be-all and end-all for evaluation. I would recommend a memory block and transformation to Nurturer phase. It can be retrained to function as a Nurturer, and I firmly believe it will make an excellent one. You've seen its intelligence ratings. Well above the minimum."

"I don't agree," another of the circle spoke up. This one was brown with a grey muzzle and markings on the chest. "Memory blocks are too tricky. Not selective enough. Besides, it's always possible that the original memory will re-emerge. In this case, I strongly suspect it will. No, the only alternatives are termination or transportation. I propose."

Greyback nodded solemnly. "Twistthought proposes. We will consider." All the Nurturers in the circle growled assent. They linked paws and closed their eyes. A steady rumble of low growling arose from their closed mouths. The rumble droned on and on, making the air and then the ground itself vibrate. Strong gazed at them in wonder. It had not understood a thing it had heard. The words were strange and had no references the Catcher could place.

Suddenly the noise stopped and the Nurturers opened their eyes. Greyback spoke first. "As eldest, I propose transportation. The bloodline is too valuable to waste."

Redfur was next. "As youngest, I propose termination. The bloodline is good, true, but the K factor is dangerously high." Around the circle it went until all nine had spoken. Five had proposed transportation, four termination.

Greyback smiled at Strong. "Made it by a whisker, young one. You're going to Home. Pity, really. I understand you were the fastest of the Chasers and the strongest of the Catchers. You'll miss the plain, mark my words. I did. Still do.

"But come. Home is better than termination. You'll be transformed again. Sorry about that. There just isn't any use for a Catcher at Home. We'll take your eggs and you'll become a Nurturer, probably the youngest ever. Later it will all be explained to you. You won't like it any better, but at least you'll understand."

Strong looked around the circle in bewilderment. "Where . . . where are you taking me?"

Greyback sighed. "I told you. Home. Though I realize it means nothing to you. Couldn't. You've always lived here on the Reserve." Seeing Strong's sudden fear and confusion, Greyback spoke softly. "Strong, you wanted to find out about the plain rising up and up, didn't you?" Strong nodded. "Well, then, you're going to. You see, Strong, we're going to take you with us. We're going to take you beyond where the plain rises."

Strong peered intently at Greyback. The Catcher knew that the Nurturer was telling the truth. A sudden elation filled Strong's chest. I'm going beyond where the plain rises into the sky! With a grin and a nod, the Catcher stepped forward eagerly.

II.

They walked across the plain for three days in a direction Strong had never been before. Whenever they came to a pack, one of the Nurturers would approach the pack to obtain food, but the others, with Strong in their midst, would go around without greetings or touchings of paws. Finally, after many weary days of walking, they came to a great jumble of rocks that stood at the top of a slight hill. In a group, with Strong in the middle, the nine Nurturers entered the pile of rocks. None of them came out the other side.

It was a dark place and it smelled strange. Smelled like the nine Nurturers. Greyback walked by Strong's side, murmuring reassurances as they walked. "Covers most of one continent," the old Nurturer said. "all four edges curve up and up. The field is generated from the top edge and it closes off the top of the Reserve so no radiation can enter. Luckily this continent wasn't hit as hard as Home was. Nothing can survive outside on the surface of Home.

"We've matched the background radiation level pretty closely to the Time of Growth. Most of the species in the Reserve are cloned from those still surviving in out-of-the-way places. Some were created from bits and pieces of those that didn't make it through the Time of Confusion. All it takes is a couple of cells that still have their DNA. The rest is easy, really.

"Of course, we didn't get a total match. Not every species is the same and not all are represented. But the differences are minor and not too important. Works out to ten decimals."

They all came to a stop and sat down. Greyback pulled Strong down. "Relax, young one. This will all seem strange. But you'll soon grow weary of it all." The floor of the area they were sitting on began to shake.

Slowly the fear left Strong's mind, and the Catcher fell asleep leaning against the grey shoulder of the old Nurturer. Greyback kept talking in a soft undertone, explaining this and that. Very few of the words made any sense awake, and none managed to penetrate Strong's sleep.

III.

Strong changed. The claws shrunk, the muscles turned to bulk. The protoeggs matured rapidly and were taken away. Then birthing pouches began to grow on Strong's stomach, and the Catcher realized it was a Catcher no more.

They trained the new Nurturer, drilling it and teaching it many things. Most were strange and often made little sense at first. Then a new bit of information would come along, and suddenly many things wondered about would make sense. The

new Nurturer's teachers were pleased with its progress and
gave it a Nurturer's name: Sure.

Greyback visited often and actually seemed to Sure to be in
charge of the education process. After more than a double turn
of seasons, the old Nurturer came one day and sat for a long
time questioning Sure. Nodding at last, fully satisfied, Greyback spoke with great solemnity. "We've taught you all we can
for now, young one. The rest all hangs on the Solution and how
we got to the point of needing it. It is time you learned
something no one has taught you, something no one on the
plain had any use for." Greyback sighed. "Would that none of
us had ever had any use for it. We call it 'history,' and it comes
to exist when a species begins to change itself and move away
from its natural condition. Ours began some one million years
ago when we first became truly sentient. Pity, that.

"I'll just give you a quick outline. Your regular teachers will
fill it in with more than enough detail." Greyback sat back and
composed itself for several moments before continuing. "Now
then," it began when ready, "it started when Nurturers,
concerned because of a vast drought that was affecting the
plain here on Home, began to become more sedentary,
gathering in more permanent settlements near secure water
sources where they could grow plant food as well as receive the
fruits of the hunt from the Catchers and the Chasers.

"Of course, as soon as they settled, hunting in the immediate
area became poorer than ever and they were forced to turn even
more to the plants they tended for sustenance. The result was
that hunting patterns changed, living patterns changed, and the
original relationships between Chaser, Catcher, and Nurturer
changed.

"Was the change for the better? Who knows. Was it
necessary? Probably not. But it seems to be a fairly common
pattern in the galaxy, repeated on many worlds.

"In any case, it led to permanent settlements. In a permanent
settlement, a Chaser isn't too valuable. A Catcher, thanks to its
strength, is valuable. But not at catching. Well, it's all very
complicated, and your teachers will give you all the ins and
outs of it. What it all comes down to is that we made a mess
of our species and nearly ended up destroying both ourselves
and our world. We made ourselves into something we were
not. We attempted to totally separate ourselves from nature and

our original condition, to create ourselves all over again by our own artifices, to restructure our species according to our own design."

The old Nurturer paused and stared at its paws for long moments. Eventually it looked up, its eyes sad. "We failed," it said softly, shrugging. It shook itself and gave a wry smile.

"Luckily, before we blew everything to pieces, we had been discovered by the Federation and had joined in order to trade. When we pulled everything down around our ears, we had a transmitter and were able to put out a call for help.

"A Questioner showed up. We were lucky. The system had been quarantined by the Federation and no one else would come. Other than pirates, of course, to plunder the ruins. But Questioners aren't affected by things like that. They go where their ships take them. And the ships are programmed for random jumps. But still, we were lucky. It could have been hundreds of years before a Questioner would have shown up by chance. Dumb luck.

"You'll learn all about the Solution when it's time. But basically it was to go back into our own past to find out why we had done what we had done. The Questioner told us to build the Reserve. It took all the manpower we had. Every survivor dedicated its life to the project. It took three generations just to finish it. And ever since then, the Reserve has been the center of our race's efforts. The Reserve and the Project.

"And what have we learned for all that time and effort? Precious little. Except one big thing. We, and we alone, have the power to save ourselves or destroy ourselves. There is no place else to go for help. The Questioner's solution to our problem was really very simple. I guess you could say it was 'You are whom you are. You will be whom you choose to be.' "

Greyback looked deep into Sure's eyes. "The Solution, young one, applies to our race. But it also applies to each and every one of us individually as well. In fact, it only applies to our race through each individual. If each one of us takes responsibility for the decision we make, and then makes the right one, the race will survive. If not . . . well, then, best we not survive. The galaxy doesn't need any more problems than it already has." Greyback patted Sure gently on the head, as if it were a mere cub. "And now, young one, I think it's time you saw something you must eventually see. You've been cooped here in these underground warrens long enough. I'm going to take you outside, onto the surface of Home. Not a very long trip. That would be deadly. Just a short one. Just so you can see what we did to ourselves. I think you're strong enough to see it. In any case, we'll soon find out. It must happen sometime. Come."

IV.

The ride on the transporter was about an hour long. An hour, Sure thought. How strange. I never even used to divide time in units this way. A day was a day and I never tried to break it up into pieces.

They reached the end of the line they were on and got out. A guard was there, a Catcher of huge proportions, and it checked both their identification tags before letting them pass. "Want suits?" it asked Greyback with a disinterested growl. The old Nurturer replied with a grunt. "No. Just a short trip. It's the Nurturer's first."

The guard nodded solemnly. "Short is best in that case. And good luck." The Catcher went to a large door, pushed several buttons, and the door opened slowly on a small chamber. They went into the chamber and sat on the bench along one wall.

"Be a few minutes," Greyback said. "Have to adjust the pressure. Higher in here than outside. You'll be a bit short of breath for a few minutes, so take it easy." The old Nurturer pointed to a red light over a door in the opposite wall from where they had entered. "When that light goes on we leave by that door. Brace yourself, Sure. You're about to see what is really beyond where the plain rises."

The light turned red and they moved across the chamber to the door. Greyback punched several buttons in an intricate pattern and the door swung back. The old Nurturer gestured for Sure to precede, and the two of them entered a narrow passage that had been cut into the rock. It led upward at a slight angle.

They walked for about three hundred yards toward a bright light that indicated the passage opened onto the planet's surface. Sure was the first to step out into the sunlight. For several moments the creature's eyes were dazzled by the bright light. Then slowly it began to make out the features of the landscape that surrounded it and rolled off to every horizon.

At first, Sure stared in confusion and incomprehension. Then suddenly it realized what it was looking at. The shapes made sense. And the horror rose swiftly. The new Nurturer felt its breath coming in quick pants. There wasn't enough air! There wasn't enough anything!

Dimly, Sure heard Greyback's voice. "This is the plain where we were born. This is what we did to it. This is what we are. This is what you are."

With a scream of anguish and despair, Sure collapsed.

The Leap

*Heaven knows what seeming nonsense may not
tomorrow be demonstrated truth.*

Alfred North Whitehead

I.

The Nurturer sat and looked off into the distance. The expression on its face was vague and dull, the mouth was slack, and a slight drool coming from the right side matted the fur on its neck. It was poorly groomed since none of the others particularly enjoyed its torpidness or its sudden flareups of random rage. It sat alone, as it usually did, and stared off into nothingness.

They had all named it Slowslow when it first wandered into the pack from somewhere on the plain. None of the other Nurturers could remember having seen it before, but that didn't matter, for it was a Nurturer and that was all anyone had to know.

Slowslow had barely been able to communicate when it had first arrived. Gradually, though, it had begun to utter simple sentences. Still, it hadn't been able to recite any of the Tales or even hold an intelligent conversation with the teachable cubs. As a result, they had entrusted it with the care of only the youngest, nonverbal cubs, the ones which had emerged from the pouches but still had to be nursed. With these tiny creatures, Slowslow was profoundly gentle and caring. It would croon tunelessly to them for hours, a vague smile on its muzzle. The cubs would sit quietly, their eyes big, gentle smiles on their faces, utterly enthralled by the sound of Slowslow's voice. It was almost as if the wordless, tuneless sound held intense and significant meaning for them.

As the years passed, Slowslow showed virtually no signs of aging. Unlike the other Nurturers, who gradually grayed and moved more and more ponderously, Slowslow's fur remained the same golden color and the creature actually seemed to become more active and filled with energy. And, surprisingly, the Nurturer gradually seemed to be growing more and more aware of its surroundings, itself, and the other members of the pack. It spoke longer and more complex sentences and even told a few Tales, though badly and confusedly.

Yet though there were marked improvements in Slowslow, the strange Nurturer stayed apart from the rest of the Nurturers and the older cubs. The younger cubs continued to adore the creature, but once they began to learn the Tales, they gradually began to shun Slowslow.

So, ungroomed, generally alone though occasionally surrounded by young cubs, it would sit and stare off toward the sunrise and croon strange, tuneless melodies.

II.

A day came when Slowslow was the oldest Nurturer in the pack. By all the rights of tradition, this gave it leadership. But Slowslow appeared utterly disinterested in such things. It spoke normally now, even told the Tales well, though it would occasionally end them in ways that were not usual; in ways that slightly distorted their meaning and disturbed the mind. Somehow, although most of the words were the traditional ones, the emphasis was different, so that the stories twisted sideways or slewed off in an unexpected direction, or even curved up when they should have simply run off flatly forever.

Surprisingly, even though the other members of the pack now more or less accepted or at least tolerated the presence of Slowslow, it still seemed to prefer the company of the youngest cubs to that of the older cubs and the other Nurturers.

There was no doubt in anyone's mind that Slowslow was strange. But it was still a shock to them all to watch early one morning as the Nurturer patted several of the younger cubs on their heads and then turned without so much as a word of goodbye or explanation to anyone else and began to walk slowly across the plain toward the rising sun.

Slowslow walked for many days, stopping briefly at every pack it met to rest and eat. Everyone was polite to it, for over the years news of this mysterious Nurturer had spread slowly across the plain from pack to pack until all had heard of it. Even a few of its own twisted versions of the Tales had passed along as well. Most shook their heads in pity as it passed, wondering what could have happened to its mind that it behaved in such a bizarre manner. Yet everywhere it went, the younger cubs swarmed to it and it would croon to them, a wide and happy smile curving its muzzle.

Eventually Slowslow came to the last pack. The area further toward the sunrise was territory belonging to no pack. It was not hunted. The Tales, especially some of the newer ones, warned against it.

No one was surprised, however, when after a few days resting with the pack, the Nurturer left one morning heading toward the sun. Chasers, Catchers, Nurturers, and even the cubs stood and watched it go, a strange sadness filling them all.

III.

Slowslow walked and walked all day and all night, not pausing to eat or sleep or even drink. There was something inside the Nurturer that drove it onward against all normal instincts, some internal pressure that grew and grew with every step toward the place where the sun rose.

It moved ponderously, slowly, but it never stopped. Foot was placed in front of foot over and over again. For two, then three days and nights it marched forward, always forward, in a straight line. There was no question it knew exactly where it was going, even if it didn't know why.

On the fourth day it stopped at a small stream to drink deeply. It took no food, even though hunger struck sharply and repeatedly at its stomach. When it had finished drinking, it stood immediately and began walking again. There was no reason to rest. There was only the place where the sun rose, calling, calling, demanding.

Then, on the fifth day, as the sun rose, Slowslow topped a slight ridge and stopped. Its eyes followed the plain out and out into the distance. Out and out. And then up. Up and up into the sky. Up until it disappeared into the clouds. It craned its neck back and stared upwards into the rising sun. A glidewing soared slowly on thermals created by the rising of the plain.

Slowslow shivered mightily as if sloughing off a heavy pelt that had been weighing it down. It threw back its head, opened its muzzled and roared.

Slowly the roaring became words. One phrase, cried out over and over. "I remember! I remember! I remember . . ."

The whole of reality can be ready in the idea; without the occasion it never becomes real.

Soren Kierkegard

I.

Seeker became dimly aware that it was being carried over the shoulder of some large creature. Fear welled up suddenly and it was fully awake in an instant. Before it could act, however, a low voice spoke to it. "Back among the living, eh?" the voice said softly, reassuringly. "I'll be glad to put you down and let you walk if you wish. You're damn heavy, especially when you're all limp!"

The ursoid recognized the voice even as it was deposited gently on the ground. Bilrog. Seeker shook its head in confusion, trying to sort things out. First the plain had risen into the sky. Then there had been overwhelming fear and darkness. And finally, waking up over Bilrog's shoulder. There didn't seem to be any logical connections between the events.

Not quite true, Seeker admitted to itself. The first two were closely and directly linked. It was only the last that . . .

"Longarm said you were out here. When you didn't come back by dark, I got worried and decided to come out after you." Bilrog had squatted down next to Seeker and was speaking softly. "Good thing, too. There were a couple of nasty things circling around you, trying to decide if they dared take a nip out of your hide, when I found you. What happened? You were out like a light. Nothing I did brought you around."

Seeker swallowed several times. "Well . . . the plain curved up and . . . oh, what's the use? You couldn't understand. It was just the shock of seeing something that I thought . . ."

"Easy, easy," Bilrog said soothingly. "You haven't been conscious all that long. Go slow. Guess I asked the wrong question. Do you think you can stand now? We really should be getting back. It's not good to stop too long in one place, especially not at night."

The ursoid looked around and realized it was indeed night. It growled a small, self-deprecating chuckle. "Guess I'm pretty much confused still. Yes, I think I can walk. Just give me your arm so I can get up. Yes. Thank you. Yes, I can stand, so I can walk."

The two of them began to walk along, side by side. Bilrog was total awareness, looking constantly from side to side, listening to every sound, sniffing every scent. After a few moments Seeker asked in a whisper, "How did you find me?"

Bilrog cast a quick look from the corner of its eye, and a crooked smile curved its mouth. "Not too hard. The plain is flat and you're not. You were the highest point for a long way around. Mount Seeker, so to speak."

Seeker chuckled. "Well, yes, Nurturers do get a little fat as they grow older. I'm young for a Nurturer and nowhere near as fat as most. But, yes, I'm not exactly flat." For a few moments Seeker walked in watchful silence, then spoke again. "I guess the real question is why you found me."

"Why?" Bilrog repeated the question. "Hmmmmm. Just seemed like the right thing to do, us being Pretenders together and all that. When Longarm told me that . . ."

A long sinuous form eruped from the darkness to the left of Bilrog. The Furmorian moved swiftly to the right, two knives flashing darkly in its fists. The action was so swift Seeker missed it. There was a sudden howl and a thud and then Bilrog was there beside the ursoid once more, speaking as if nothing had happened. ". . . you had run into some trouble out on the plain, I decided I'd best see if you needed any help."

"I did," Seeker said. "Thank you very much." Bilrog shrugged and then continued on for a long time before the furmorian said gently, "Darkhider died. Longarm tried to save the little lizard, but its wounds were too serious."

Seeker sighed. "I'd grown rather fond of Darkhider. I'm sorry to hear that. First Thisunit, then Darkhider. I wonder who's next? Huh. Guess I almost was. How is H*mb*1?"

Bilrog cocked its head to one side and gave Seeker a quick glance. "I was hoping you might have seen the hummer. I haven't had sight of it for at least two days. It hasn't come back to Start that I know of."

The ursoid felt a chill. "Then H*mb*1 must be dead, too."

"No," Bilrog said quietly, "I don't think so. Neither does Longarm."

Sudden hope flared up in Seeker. "Do you think H*mb*1 could have made it to Sanctuary? Of all of us, the hummer always seemed the most likely one to make it to me."

The Furmorian chuckled. "No, I don't think H*mb*1 has found Sanctuary yet. Longarm doesn't think so either. Perhaps . . ."

There was a motion ahead of them and they both froze in place. Something was moving toward them, smoothly, silently, subtly. Tensely, they both stood stock still and waited for the night to reveal it.

When the shape finally appeared, they both laughed out loud with relief. "Speak of the cub and it pounces!" Seeker said. "H*mb*1, we were just wondering where you were, and here you appear out of the . . ." The ursoid's voice ran down to silent amazement and wonder. The thing that danced slowly toward them and then around them was H*mb*1. And yet again it wasn't.

"H*mb*1?" Bilrog asked in a strange, strangled voice.

The dancing figure failed to reply. It began to hum softly, wordlessly as it danced around them once, then twice. Then, without further pausing or even acknowledging their existence, the dancer disappeared into the night.

The two stood and stared at each other for a long time. Finally Bilrog nodded and said, "Well, we know what happened to H*mb*1. In a strange way I guess the hummer did find Sanctuary."

"What happened?" Seeker said, its voice echoing its confusion. "It was H*mb*1 but it wasn't. It didn't even notice us. It . . ."

"Oh, I think it noticed us. And included us in its dance for a brief moment. But there are bigger dances here on Labyrinth, and I think the hummer is dancing the biggest of them all."

Seeker looked dismayed. "What do you mean?"

"Ask Longarm when we get back to Start. Maybe the Teacher can explain. But if we don't get moving, we might not get a chance to ask any questions at all. Things are gathering, drawn by our scent and our talking. We have to move, fast. Let's go."

They began to run with Bilrog in the lead. Seeker followed, its mind a turmoil of questions and possible answers.

II.

"Sanctuary?" Longarm laughed. "H*mb*1 has no need of Sanctuary. Creatures like you and Bilrog, you need Sanctuary. But not H*mb*1."

"But H*mb*1 can't just wander endlessly out there!" Seeker said angrily. "Sooner or later something will get the hummer and kill it! We've got to go help!"

Longarm laughed even more loudly. "Help H*mb*1? Help yourself, Seeker. But don't bother H*mb*1. The hummer doesn't need anyone's help."

Seeing the ursoid's confusion, the Teacher smiled and said, "Look, Seeker, H*mb*1 is safe out there, safer than it would be anywhere in the galaxy."

"But how can that be?" Seeker asked worriedly. "Labyrinth is the deadliest place in the galaxy and . . ."

Longarm held up a hand to stop the ursoid. "Deadly to those who have a purpose. But H*mb*1 no longer has a purpose. Indeed, in one way there isn't really any H*mb*1 to have a purpose any more."

Seeker sighed deeply and shook its head. "I don't understand. I just don't understand."

"Well," the Teacher began, "look at it this way. Sentience, which is always self-consciousness, has a purpose, an end toward which it strives. That's its nature, that's why it evolves and develops. The end isn't just something for the purpose of something else and that for something else and so on to infinity. That would be circular, endless, and futile. No, sentience always aims at the same thing in every species it develops in. Its goal is always the happiness of the individual sentient being, whether a single being or a group being of some kind, in terms of the optimum functioning of the individual within the parameters of its possibilities. So sentience is always dynamic, always reaching out toward possibility.

"The result is that sentience is both creative and destructive. It seeks to transform the world around it and mold it to its own ends, the ends of happiness and a happy life. Some species end up destroying both themselves and their planets in the process. Others do better.

"Labyrinth is sentient. Hence, the planet as a whole seeks its own happiness. That means that any other sentients on its face inevitably come into conflict with it, because they are seeking their own happiness, and their version of their happiness and the planet's version of its are bound to be different. For that reason, it tries to kill them."

Longarm looked up at Seeker from under beetling brows and chuckled. "Follow it all so far? Eh? Good, good. And what does this all have to do with H*mb*1, you wonder? Well, follow along a bit further.

"H*mb*1, like all Pretenders, came here seeking something. And like all Pretenders, it was a personal vision of happiness somehow related to becoming a Questioner. You'd be surprised, by the way, at the number of different reasons for wanting to become a Questioner. In all my years as a Teacher, I don't remember ever hearing two alike, not even from members of the same species.

"The point, though, is that such a seeking after happiness is exactly what Labyrinth will react against. So by the very act of coming here with a goal, that of becoming a Questioner, the planet tries to kill you. Something of a paradox, I admit, but that's the way life is.

"H*mb*1 found itself caught in the paradox. To keep Labyrinth from wanting to kill it, it had to drop its own ends. That is, to succeed, it had to cease wanting to succeed. Not just pretend to cease wanting to succeed, but really and truly to infinitely resign all attempts at success. But if it did that, then what was the purpose for being here in the first place?

"The hummer finally decided. It was here to dance and for nothing else. The dance, since it has no goal other than merely dancing what is there without changing or influencing it in any way, does not run contrary to the interests of Labyrinth in any way. Hence there is no conflict and the planet no longer wants to kill the dancer. By merging with the dance, H*mb*1 in a sense merges with the planet and loses all purpose by infinitely resigning it.

"So, Seeker, there is no reason to worry about your friend. It is in no danger. It will dance the face of Labyrinth forever without any harm ever befalling it."

"But . . . but it won't ever become a Questioner, will it? I mean, if it just dances forever . . ."

Longarm nodded. "You're right, of course. H*mb*1 is only halfway to becoming a Questioner. It has made the first movement, that of infinite resignation. To become a Questioner, though, requires a second movement, one so difficult it is almost impossible to describe, much less make. But I'll try.

"You see, once the move of infinite resignation is made, once all purpose is allowed to dissolve away from one, then the only way to regain purpose is to believe it will happen in spite of the obvious impossibility of its happening. I don't just mean that it is unlikely that it will happen, for then there would still be a slight hope of purpose and the resignation wouldn't be infinite. No, hope must be utterly given up and the regaining of purpose utterly impossible. But at the same time, the Pretender must be utterly certain it will succeed, that it will achieve its purpose fully and completely right here on the face of Labyrinth."

"But . . . but that's absurd!" Seeker protested.

"Yes," Longarm nodded with a smirk. "Utterly, totally, wonderfully absurd."

"Crazy," the ursoid muttered.

"Crazy, too. And stupid and ridiculous and impossible and . . . oh, a whole host of things. But that's the way it is here on Labyrinth, Seeker. There's no way around it and no way to get to Sanctuary except through the very center of the paradox."

Seeker frowned and shook its head in exasperation. "There's nothing to get hold of! Everything twists and turns and slips away just as I think I begin to understand." The ursoid looked beseechingly at Longarm. "I just don't understand it, Teacher."

Longarm smiled. "That's the problem. You want to understand it, but there's nothing to understand."

The ursoid growled softly with frustration. "But it must all mean something! All these deaths. Thisunit. Darkhider. And H*mb*1, for all intents and purposes. Answer me that at least, Teacher! Why are all these deaths necessary? Couldn't Labyrinth accomplish what it wants without killing?"

The Teacher looked thoughtfully at Seeker. "All these deaths? You have no concept of how many creatures have died here on Labyrinth. The planet is almost as old as the galaxy, maybe older. And all that time, Labyrinth has been doing what it is doing now. We're not talking about two creatures dying, or even two hundred thousand. We're talking of billions of deaths. Billions."

"But why? What purpose can all this death serve?"

Longarm shrugged. "Perhaps no other purpose than to teach us that mortality rather than sentience is the essence of existence."

Seeker blinked and looked confused. "But how can death be the essence of existence? The two contradict each other."

The Teacher sighed. "Seeker, when is it possible to write one's true autobiography?"

"Why . . . why . . . when one's life is complete, I guess."

"And when is that?"

Seeker stared at the Teacher, comprehension dawning in its eyes. "When one dies."

Longarm nodded. "Yes, for before the moment of death, any life's meaning can be utterly changed by one last event. For that reason, true autobiography can never be written. Only a sort of report on a life in progress is possible.

"Death, Seeker, is not something that happens to us in our life. It is not just one more possibility among others. Rather, death is the horizon of all the things we do. All potential, all possibility, is grounded in the future. And that is where death always is. It is an ultimate event that never arrives because we cease to exist as it happens, so we can't experience it. We experience dying, but never death. It cannot be outstripped since it outstrips all other possibilities. It contains life, acts as the mould of life, the horizon toward which life strives. It is not within life, but rather contains life within it. It locates all other possibilities and potentials, not as a simple event, which it never is, but as the ultimate possibility and potential."

"But . . . but . . . " Seeker stammered in confusion, "death is the end of life, the stopping of time and being . . ."

Longarm smiled. "On the contrary. Death is not doom, but rather the very thing that makes life and striving possible. Death is the structure that underlies life and makes potentiality conceivable. Death, rather than birth, is the driving force of life. Think of a spring, Seeker, gushing up out of the ground. At first thought, the spring seems to be the origin of the river, and time seems to flow from the past, as the water wells up, toward the future, as it runs down toward the sea. But why does the water flow? Because of the upwelling, or because of the seeking of the ocean? If it was the upwelling, then there would be no reason for the water to flow anywhere. No, it is the seeking, the possibility of its end that the water flows toward. So it is with life.

"Time, Seeker, is not projection from the present back into the past and forward into the future. Nor is it discovered as a memory of what has happened to one. Instead time is found as projection forward, as future, as possibility, as the movement toward the horizon which is death."

Seeker felt its mind reeling. "If we move toward death, why move at all?"

The Teacher nodded slightly and replied, "Yes, indeed, why? In the very midst of life we find ourselves in death. The first cry of the newborn is but the beginning of the death rattle. Why strive, seek, struggle? Why not simply sit and wait for what will come anyway?"

Longarm shrugged and chuckled. "Oh, the many ways we hide death from ourselves in an attempt to make life transcendent! We celebrate the deaths of others, make the event into a thing that can be denied because we push it away and say it belongs to that other, the dead one, but surely not to us. The grander the ceremony, the more assurance that the other is dead and we are not. Or we create myths of realms that transcend our own where we go after death, so that death becomes a mere transition rather than a horizon, a mere passage to a wider world. Or we deny its necessity and search for immortality. We hide it, obfuscate it, deny it. And then . . . we die."

"But Darkhider and Thisunit . . ."

"Their death was not yours. Yours is not theirs. You go toward your future even as they went toward theirs. Your future, Seeker, your potential, your possibility. The primary meaning of your existence is the future. And the future is death.

"Your very existence, Seeker, is an existence toward death. But if you fear death and refuse to move toward it, you stagnate and cease to grow or realize your possibilities. And then you die anyway."

Seeker stared blankly at the dusty ground. After several moments it raised stricken eyes to the Teacher and murmured, "I . . . I just don't understand. I can't seem to figure out what to do. There just doesn't seem to be any hope for me. I . . . I'll never become a Questioner."

"Most likely," Longarm said with a smug grin. "But then, it's entirely up to you."

III.

Seeker spent several days in Start recuperating. Then several more trying to work up the courage to go back out onto the face of Labyrinth. Every morning Bilrog greeted the ursoid with a cheery hello before it left to wander, with apparent nonchalance and immunity, wherever whim took it.

Seeker's first trip out was a tentative one that ended early in the day when it came across H*mb*1 dancing with a giant spider. For several moments the ursoid stood and watched the dance in wonder and horror. The horror got the upper hand and Seeker fled back to the safety of Start, its heart beating wildly and its knees feeling watery and weak.

Eventually, though, it returned to the plain where it had previously collapsed. The plain still rose into the sky in the distance, but Seeker realized the rising must be some sort of bizarre optical illusion, for the closer it walked to the upthrust, the more it receded into the distance.

It felt vaguely at home on the plain, and memory came crowding into its mind. Swift running after game. Strong grabbing and killing it with incredible power. Sure studying the history of its people in the city beneath the ground. Slowslow plodding, mind empty, drooling.

Seeker remembered how memory had returned to Slowslow as it had stood there watching the plain rise toward the sky. With memory had come a hot anger as it remembered what had been done to it. The anger had soon become cold and purposeful and the Nurturer had headed for the pile of rocks it knew dotted the plain. There it had called the transporter to it and had returned to the underground city on Home.

Slowslow's appearance in the city caused quite a stir. When it discovered that Greyback had died long ago, Slowslow demanded to see some other member of the Council. The Nurturer that finally met with Slowslow was none other than a very old and slivery Redfur. The ancient Nurturer looked Slow slow up and down distastefully and muttered, "I was right about termination, bloodline or not. You've been nothing but trouble since the day we created you. How did you escape the mindblock?"

"Time," Slowslow said softly. "Time, and something inside me you couldn't block no matter how hard you tried."

Redfur snorted. "I voted termination the second time, too, after you collapsed up on the surface. Weak. Unbalanced mind. A K factor too high for stability. But Greyback had his way again, five to four again. Wanted your bloodline."

The grizzled Nurturer looked Slowslow over and sighed. "Well, here you are. What are we supposed to do with you?"

"Continue my teaching. I want to learn everything. The thing you couldn't kill in me, that thing was my desire to know."

"I'm aware of that," Redfur answered sharply, petulantly. "That's what K factor is. Damned curiosity. Damned desire to constantly be poking into things, to discover something new." The old Nurturer's voice rose in anger. "K factor is what drove us on and on and led to what we did, the destruction, everything!"

"It didn't have to lead there," Slowslow said with quiet assurance. "We chose to take it there, but it didn't have to be that way. That is the lesson the Questioner really was trying to teach us, Redfur. That's why we were supposed to set up the Reserve, to give ourselves a chance to let our desire to learn run in the right paths instead of the wrong, destructive ones.

The Questioner was trying to give us a second chance to use our reasoning powers, our sentience, for positive ends."

"Sentience is a curse!" Redfur growled. "The Reserve is to help us breed it out of our race, to return to what we were before we started asking questions. It was to . . ."

"Too late," Slowslow interrupted. "I've seen what the surface of Home looks like. It's too late to go back. We can only go forward. I want to learn more so I can help find the way. That's why I've come back. Let me learn."

Redfur sighed deeply. "I'm old, old, old. I don't care all that much any more. My time of darkness is nearby, just over the next rise. Do what you will. You are a fool bred from fools. You will find nothing here. It is too late. The Questioner saved us only from imminent doom. Our fate still stalks us and will be on us soon again. It was a temporary reprieve and it was not enough."

Seeker brought its mind back to the present with an effort. It looked around to make sure nothing hostile or deadly was in the area. This is Labyrinth, after all, the ursoid reminded itself. Yet here on the plain everything seemed safe, and Seeker felt secure. It realized that in all the time it had been here, no physical danger had ever threatened it.

The ursoid paused for a second as a new thought slipped into its mind. Perhaps Labyrinth was attacking in a different manner. What if the lack of hostile creatures was simply a sign that the war was being waged on a different level? And what level would that be?

The answer was obvious. Longarm had once indicated that the planet attacked the mind and the spirit as well as the body. Could Labyrinth's new assault be mental?

Seeker thought of the optical illusion of the plain curving up and how the sight had almost unhinged its mind. It thought of the doubt that Longarm constantly tried to sow in its mind. And it thought of the constant series of memories that flooded into its consciousness every time it came out here on the plain. Could its own mind be the new battlefield?

It seemed only too possible. After all, Seeker realized, it was my mind that caused all the trouble back on the real plain and in the underground city on Home. After I came back for the second time, I plunged into my studies with a fervor that shocked even the most dedicated teachers. And I asked endless questions on every imaginable topic. Which was how I got my new name, Seeker.

It wasn't long before most of the teachers began to avoid contact with Seeker. The Nurturer spent all of its time in the data collections, poring over every piece of information it could find. Its knowledge grew and grew until some of the teachers began to realize that Seeker had long ago surpassed them in the sheer quantity of things it knew.

Then one day, unexpectedly, it all came crashing down. The amount of material studied had piled deeper and deeper until it simply collapsed under its own weight. Wildly Seeker tried to organize it all, to stabilize it by placing it in some kind of overall, coherent framework. But the task was hopeless.

The confusion and resulting madness lasted for several years. Then, once again as on the plain with Slowslow, Seeker won out and came back. But this time it was a saddened and chastened creature that greeted the world. A creature that had begun to wonder to the very depths of its being if understanding was truly attainable.

And if understanding wasn't possible, what was left? For several years Seeker pondered that thought while taking long walks across the hideous, ruined face of Home. The final decision was one that had surprised everyone.

Seeker shook its head again. Drifting! Slipping into the past. But at least this time the memories had brought it back into the present. Yes, Seeker thought, I came here to Labyrinth hoping to learn something. And have I?

The ursoid looked around, nervously checking its surroundings for danger. The plain was empty. There was nothing to fear. Have I learned anything? Seeker wondered. Yes, at least one thing. The pain of uncertainty is as universal as sentience itself.

IV.

Bilrog smiled slightly as Seeker got up and began to move again. The Furmorian was hidden from the view of the ursoid, not that Seeker was particularly observant of late, but the warrior was still close enough to reach the other Pretender's side in a flash if danger threatened.

Shouldn't you be worrying about yourself? the inner voice asked. Bilrog chuckled. Plenty of time for that later. Right now it was Seeker that was in danger. Labyrinth was messing with its mind and Seeker was simply so absorbed with the mental struggle that it was unaware of the dangerous physical things that stalked it. Unaware because Bilrog had intercepted every one of them and dispatched them before they ever reached the distracted ursoid.

Why? the voice asked. Because, Bilrog replied, Seeker needs help right now. And you don't? the voice queried. Not really, Bilrog answered. What about finding Sanctuary? Isn't that the reason you're here? What happened to finding Sanctuary?

Bilrog smiled broadly. Oh, I know where Sanctuary is. I can get there any time I want. The Furmorian chuckled again. Right now Seeker needs help. I can always get to Sanctuary later, after the issue is decided with Seeker.

The issue? the voice wondered. Aye, Bilrog said. The issue of whether Seeker will succeed or fail. It's coming to a head soon. It won't be much longer. Then I can go to Sanctuary alone or with Seeker. We'll see, we'll see.

V.

The poisontooth came at Seeker with such speed that the ursoid didn't see it until it was almost too late. At the last moment it spun away and slashed outward and raked the side of the beast with razor-sharp claws. The poisontooth turned to make a second attack but the legs on the slashed side refused to work properly and it collapsed in a heap.

Crusharm came in a rage, claws flashing, teeth bared. They circled for a while, trading blows, ripping bits of fur and flesh from each other. Then Crusharm was on its knees and Seeker was in like a flash, striking downward. The gore splattered in every direction. Crusharm tried to rise but the blood gushed from its throat and it tumbled to the ground.

Redfur was at Seeker's mercy. Seeker slashed and bit and rended until the old Nurturer was dead.

NO! It couldn't be that way! That was the way that had led to the Time of Confusion. Retrace the steps. Change the path.

But how to change? How to act according to right reason as a true sentient should? Could it be done by changing the nature of the race? But if it was changed, would it still be the same race?

Thinking wasn't the issue. Action was. How to act rightly, in accordance with reason. There was a part of Seeker that had no notion of reason. It simply grew, mindless, without words or need of words. This part Seeker shared in common with all life on its world, plants, animals, all life.

Then there was another part, one that hungered and desired. Sometimes it used words and responded to them. Sometimes it didn't. Plants had no such part, but other animals did.

The third part sat and thought and considered and chose. It was the part Seeker shared with nothing else on its planet, the part that set it apart forever from other forms of life. It was the part that made the ursoids sentient. And even this part was divided, for one part of it pondered what goals were worthy of attainment while the other part prudently determined what means to use to achieve those goals. And wasn't there even another part, a part that tried to penetrate right to the very heart of existence and meaning, a part that wondered and wondered and sought in some way to find the source of all sentience?

But this was going too far. Seeker had to deal with the question of action in the everyday world, of how to act in the best way in any given situation. That was the issue that faced every sentient and the issue on which its race had foundered in the Time of Confusion.

There was no problem with the first part, it just did things instinctively. Nor was there any problem with the third, for it was simply thought, and thought by itself wasn't action and didn't do things.

It was the second part that created the problem. Sometimes the passions that boiled and swirled within it listened to reason and sometimes those passions overpowered even the wisest counsels. How to control it?

Pure thinking wouldn't do it. The passions were just too strong to be overcome by thought on a regular basis. Now and then it was possible, when the passion that thought tried to rule was mild or weak. But the more powerful passions didn't always respond to reason, especially not when the reasoning took time to think things through to arrive at a solution. The passions were too immediate, too demanding of instant action for thought to always remain in charge. So thought needed some kind of ally, something that had the immediacy and power of passion itself. But what could that be?

Seeker thought about the problematical part. Passion and desire were a constant search for pleasure and a constant avoidance of pain. This part of Seeker learned what gave pleasure and what yielded pain through experience and then sought to recreate those experiential situations as often as possible. If the experiences of this part could be controlled so that it could be taught to connect pleasure with those things which led to the proper results and pain with those that lead to improper ones, then . . .

But it would have to begin with the smallest cubs. The Tales would all have to be rewritten to reflect . . .

The poisontooth came at Seeker with unexpected speed. The ursoid barely had time to step aside. The creature turned and charged again. Seeker twirled out of the way with a growl of pleasure. Sport! Again and again the poisontooth charged and Seeker avoided it until finally the exhausted creature simply snarled defiance and walked away.

Crusharm was in a rage. Seeker walked away and only much later came back to talk calmly and sensibly to the other Catcher. They eventually became fast friends.

Redfur sat next to Seeker and the two discussed the things they both sought answers to.

NO! It cannot be that way. That is the way for saints, and we are ordinary beings. Sentients, not saints. There must be a middle way.

There must.

VI.

Longarm sneered. "Why must there be a way?"

"Because sentience is sacred," Seeker protested. "If there is no way, then what is the purpose of sentience?"

"Who ever said it has to have a purpose?"

"But . . . but . . . so much pain, so much desire . . ."

Longarm hooted loud laughter. "Since when did the amount of effort put forth guarantee victory? Or relevance? Just because someone writes a book of ten volumes doesn't make it more worthy than one of ten pages. Or ten words. You confuse the fact that sentience exists with the idea that it exists for some purpose beyond itself. You look for some overarching end, some universal good that sentience can achieve. No such thing is necessary or required."

"But then why does sentience exist?" Seeker cried in despair.

"Perhaps only to ask that question," Longarm replied.

VII.

Labyrinth is in my mind, Seeker whimpered to itself. In my mind, driving me somewhere, for some reason. Why? To kill me? All this effort to kill me?

Swift ran toward the place where the sun rose and saw the plain rising into the sky. The Chaser continued running until it came to the rise itself. There was a door among the rocks. It opened the door and stepped through.

All around was desolation, charred horror, bones, death. The memory, the racial memory of it all, came crashing down and Swift tried to flee. The Chaser ran across the devastation, puffs of dust and corruption rising from the ground every time its feet touched. It tried to rise into the sky to escape the violated earth, the ruined plain, the skeletons of Crusharm and the rotting carcass of Redfur. Greyback called. Swift looked up. The old Nurturer was rotting, a carcass filled with corruption.

Swift screamed and leapt higher. The glidewings soared above with utter indifference. Swift stretched out its arms to fly, to soar . . . and then crashed into the charred ruins.

Potentiality, possibility. It was not enough, not enough.

To be a Nurturer, that was actuality, possibility realized. It was commitment to the future of the race, a living for the cubs and the pack. But was growing these plants securing the future or changing it? They had never been grown in the past, and yet the future had always come. Would it come the same way now? Did a change in the present alter the future? What was the true relation between what was and what might be?

There was a place beyond actuality. It was a new possibility, one that was not fraught with the vagueness and uncertainty of before, but which was sure and certain if only one had the strength and vision to reach out and take it.

But to reach out, to lean far out over the void, to slip and fall and fall and fall . . . No. It was a leap. A leap into a possibility. A leap from the secure actuality into what? The inconceivable, the unknowable, the absurd impossibility.

Labyrinth is in my mind!!!! Why???????
Justkillmejustkillmejustkillmejustkillmejustkillmeeeeeeeee.

Silence. Darkness. Is this death?

VIII.

The days came and went without counting, without number, without meaning. Seeker wandered the plain listlessly. The real battle was elsewhere, on a plain that never existed. Bilrog followed, though now nothing dangerous ever appeared to trouble the wanderings of the ursoid.

There was really nothing for the Furmorian to do. Nothing to say, nothing to offer, nothing to protect against. Yet the warrior stayed always within a few feet of the ursoid, always there if needed for any reason. Bilrog's expression was one of mixed hope and sadness. Seeker was obviously suffering horribly. It almost never ate and the skin was hanging from its frame in loose folds. Bilrog wasn't sure how much longer it could continue in this way. Sooner, rather than later, it would die of starvation.

Now and then Longarm came out onto the plain to watch Seeker. The Teacher would grin and scratch itself, make a few derogatory comments as though trying to jog Seeker back to consciousness, and then walk away muttering worriedly under its breath. "You're asking too much," Bilrog heard it mutter once. "Kill it or show it the way. Too much, too much."

But Seeker did not die. The ursoid struggled on across the

plain, always heading toward the place in the distance where it
seemed to rise into the sky.

They came in low over the short range of hills, hiding from
the detectors. The settlement was just on the other side of the
hills, and they were so low that the Chaser could look down
and see the faces of the pack that dwelt there as it dropped its
load of explosives into their midst. One of the heads that was
blown upwards looked very much like the Nurturer that had
borne it and raised it from cubhood.

There were too few of them left alive. The squad had started
out with a full complement of Catchers. Now there were three
left. True, they were the toughest, with the biggest muscles and
the sharpest claws, but the enemy outnumbered them ten to one
and would bury them beneath sheer numbers. Claws slashed
and sprayed blood in every direction. Cubs, mere cubs, threw
themselves at the invaders, to be smashed aside into huddled
ruins. Eventually, though, they were overpowered and every
one of the Catchers was torn to ribbons.

There was no end to it, the Nurturer thought. It watched the
newest batch of Chasers climb into their machines. Barely out
of cubhood. Not ready to hunt. Certainly not ready to kill. So
few would survive to become Catchers. And then they would
be sent out as infantry to invade and hold pack areas. Fewer yet
would return and mature into Nurturers. Where would it end?

They huddled in fear and despair around the transmitter.
"For the sake of sanity, send the message!" one of the
Nurturers cried. "There's no hope it will ever be answered,"
another moaned. "We've been quarantined. There aren't any
ships in the area."

"Doesn't matter," a third growled. "There's always a chance
a Questioner will come by. It's our only hope. We *must* hold
this position at all costs. And keep on sending . . ."

"Our only hope," they murmured in unison, "our only
hope."

IX.

Seeker opened its eyes and stared up at the morning light. The stillness was almost stunning. The ursoid sat up and looked around. Bilrog sat nearby. "Bilrog?" Seeker asked.

"The one and only genuine Furmorian warrior in the universe, at your service. How, um, do you feel, Seeker?"

Seeker smiled weakly. "Not very good. Sick. Empty." It looked down at its body. Surprise registered on its face. "I'm . . . I'm . . . How long has it been since I've eaten?"

Bilrog paused, considering. "Ummmm, I make it about ten days. Yes, at least that long."

"Where am I?"

"On the plain. But very close to its edge, I think." The Furmorian gestured behind Seeker and the ursoid turned around. In the near foreground, the plain rose up into the sky.

When the ursoid turned to face Bilrog once more, its eyes were wide with wonder. "Then it isn't just an optical illusion?"

"It is in a way. The rising always seems just ahead, maybe half a day. In truth, it's a good ten-day hike. But it's there all the same."

Seeker turned and looked at it again. "Yes. Yes, it's there all the same. I always knew it was. I should have gone that very first time and touched it, known for sure." The ursoid turned back to Bilrog. "But that probably wouldn't have changed a thing. No. It still would have happened the same way.

"There was never any choice, Bilrog. Never. The plain rose into the sky, and once I had seen it there was never any choice."

The Furmorian smiled gently. "There's always a choice. It's just that some are harder to make and stick to than others. But there's always a choice."

"I don't know." Seeker shook its head. "I don't know, and I'm not sure it makes any difference. I think perhaps we were all wrong, Greyback, Redfur, me. The Questioner didn't really solve our problem. Didn't even intend to. It realized we were hopeless and just gave us a breathing space, a few more centuries of life until we destroyed ourselves again."

"Perhaps the breathing space was given so you could solve your problem yourselves."

"That's what I thought once. So did Greyback. And even Redfur's approach was based on that belief. But now I wonder. Isn't it . . . isn't it possible that there are some problems that just can't be solved?"

"I'm not sure that's the right question, Seeker. Perhaps the real issue is whether or not there are any problems that *can* be solved."

Seeker shook its head wearily. "I don't know. Maybe problems can only be lived with and not solved. But I think once, a long time ago it seems now, I hoped to come here and discover the answer to my race's dilemma. I believed that here, where the Questioners themselves come from, I could find an answer to what our Questioner had tried to do for us. What had it hoped to accomplish? But now I'm no longer sure it thought that way at all."

The ursoid sighed deeply, then gave a low, self-deprecating growl. "At this moment, however, I fear I'm faced with a far simpler and more immediate problem, one that must be solved and solved soon if I'm to survive at all."

"Sanctuary?"

Seeker nodded. "I know where it is now. Right on the other side of that." The ursoid pointed behind it toward where the plain rose into the sky. "It's always been there.

"The problem is that there's something else there, too."

Bilrog nodded slowly. "Yes, I know. The abyss."

Seeker sighed. "The abyss. The bottomless nothing. There's no way across it, is there?"

"None."

"And yet I must cross it to reach Sanctuary."

"Yes."

The ursoid chuckled. "That's what Longarm was referring to, wasn't it? The absurd?"

"More or less," Bilrog answered.

"More or less," Seeker echoed. "You cannot cross the abyss because its very existence is created by the need to leap across it. The need for the leap is based on hope, and it is hope itself that makes the abyss infinite. One must abandon all hope and yet make the leap filled with hope. The energy has to come from someplace. It's a big jump."

Bilrog looked calmly at the ursoid. "Will you jump?"

Seeker laughed harshly. "It seems I have no choice. There is no hope in any direction I travel. I've lost so much weight I doubt I'd even make it back to Start alive. At least in this direction there is utter despair as well as no hope. That's something. Yes, I'll make the leap."

The ursoid rose and turned away from Bilrog and toward the rising plain. "If you ever see H*mb*1," Seeker said over its shoulder, "tell the hummer that I loved it. It won't understand, but that doesn't matter, does it?"

"Tell it yourself," Bilrog replied.

Seeker laughed. "Aye. And thanks for your confidence and for guarding me all this time. And when you get to Sanctuary, say hello to Longarm for me."

Without another word, Seeker strode off toward the rising plain. Bilrog stood and watched the ursoid until it was out of sight. Then the Furmorian turned and began to walk slowly, thoughtfully, back toward Start.

Temporality, finitude—that is what it is all about.

Soren Kierkegaard

I.

Seeker stood in a place that wasn't. There was nothing to see or hear or smell or feel though the ursoid knew it was still capable of doing all. This is not death, it thought. Nor is it life. It is nowhere/somewhere/before/after/life/death.

And I am not alone.

There was a presence, a pressure on the mind, a something in this somewhere/somewhen. It belonged here, was here.

Do you know where you are? it asked.

No, Seeker responded.

You are beyond where the plain rises up to meet the sky, came the answer.

Not really, Seeker said. The plain is an artifact, built by my people. The only thing beyond it is death, destruction, the rubble and ruins of a shattered civilization. Our civilization. The one we shattered. I've seen what it looks like on Home. It's nothing like this.

And yet you are beyond where the plain rises to meet the sky, came the voice.

Is this the abyss? Seeker asked.

The abyss is within you, came the answer.

Then am I within myself?

You are always within yourself. And that is what lies beyond the place where the plain rises.

So then I am the ruins.

You are the twisted, tortured land, the rocks that ran like water, the flesh that puffed into air, the bones that powdered to dust, the screams that evaporated unheard, unheeded, the anguish of death that fell and rose, the . . .

The love, the feeling of happiness that comes from chasing game, Seeker interrupted. The power of a clean sweep of the claws. The feeling of a young cub cuddled in your arms as it drifts to sleep. The joy of placing a ripe egg in your pouch. The joy of sunrise and sunset . . .

Yes, the voice replied softly, yes, that too. For once upon a time that was also beyond where the plain rose.

But no more, Seeker said sadly.

No more. Never again.

There is no second chance?

No. What is done is done.

Was there a first chance?

See for yourself.

The cub whimpered softly. It was hungry. The Catchers had killed no game for three days now. All the cubs were hungry, as were all the Nurturers and Catchers and Chasers.

Every morning the Chasers went out and scoured the plain. But there was nothing. All the game had disappeared. No one knew why. It had never happened before.

The Nurturer cuddled the cub gently and crooned softly to it. The tiny thing fretted and squirmed, weaker than it had been yesterday. Tomorrow it would be weaker yet. The day after. . . Two of the very youngest cubs had already died. There would be more stiff little bodies to place under rocks before long.

The cub hung on for three days. It was a strong little creature and would doubtless have made a fine Chaser. But it died in the evening of the third day even as the sun was setting in a purplish haze on the horizon.

After burying it, the Nurturer stood in silence and gazed at the rock which covered it. I would have told you all the Tales, it said to itself, addressing the memory of the cub that still lived in its heart. I would have related how Speed, the greatest

Chaser of them all, had flown once, barely touching the hilltops with the tips of its claws. You would have heard the Tale of Power, the first of all the Catchers, a creature who could fell a hornhead with one mighty blow.

More cubs died. The Nurturers sat and talked. This had to be understood. And something had to be done.

So it had to be? Seeker asked.

Had to be? No, it wasn't a necessity. Had the Nurturers waited a few years, the game would have come back. Of course, by then there would have been no cubs left and your numbers would have been few. But in a hundred years you could have rebuilt.

And what's to say it wouldn't have happened again?

Nothing. There are no guarantees. But that wasn't the whole thing. There was more.

"I tell you they are a dangerous group!"

The others on the Council looked down at the ground between them. None wished to respond to Speakstrong. Finally Grizzlebeard mumbled, "But what would you have us do with them? They are our own, our Chasers, our . . .

"They are irresponsible fools!" Speakstrong said angrily. "They no longer have any function. There is no game to chase. So they spend all their time thinking up ways to cause trouble . . ."

"But they are young!" Twisthand protested. "Most have yet to develop their first protoegg."

"They must be controlled, young or not," Speakstrong declared. "We must find ways to channel their energy."

Slowthought nodded. "Yes. Cubs are no problem. Catchers are no problem. Only the Chasers are a problem. Perhaps we should keep them cubs longer and then quickly make their protoeggs mature so that they can become Catchers."

Grizzlebeard looked disturbed. "That is unnatural. Besides, we can't do such a thing."

Speakstrong growled with pleasure. "We *couldn't* do such a thing before. But now we can. My researches have paid off and we now have a way of forcing the protoeggs to mature very rapidly."

Grizzlebeard was aghast. "You'd . . . you'd change Chasers?"

"Why not?" Speakstrong shrugged. "They are nothing but a problem as they are."

"But . . . but . . . what will it do to them?"

"Change them. I already said that."

Grizzlebeard growled in anger. "That's not what I meant, and you know it. What will it do to them? What will happen to their minds, to their spirits? You change their bodies and think that is all there is to it. But you are changing far more and I doubt you have any ideas what will happen."

"I don't care. We can do this thing now. Therefore we should do it. We must progress and move forward along the path we chose many centuries ago. This must be." Speakstrong glared its challenge at Grizzlebeard.

The old Nurturer looked around the Council, trying to catch the eyes of the other members. None would look up. "Then the rest of you are willing to do this terrible thing? Willing to change ourselves to fit a new way of living? Willing to . . ." It broke off and stood up. "There is no need of me on this Council. I disagree with everything you stand for. I am old now and remember many of the old ways, ways that have come down through the years in the Tales . . ."

"We will change the Tales," Speakstrong growled.

Grizzlebeard looked down its muzzle at Speakstrong. "You will change the Tales. You will change the Chasers. You will change everything. And when you are done, who knows what you will have?" Without another word, Grizzlebeard turned and walked away from the Council, away and out onto the vast plain that stretched out and out to meet the horizon in every direction.

The others watched Grizzlebeard's departure from the corners of their eyes. Then they began to plan how they would accomplish the changing of the troublesome Chasers.

There were many places.

Yes. Many places where a slightly different action could have changed many things.

But, Seeker wondered, would it have changed the most important thing?

* * *

"We must strike swiftly and without mercy!" Swiftclaw cried. "We have tried everything else and now only force will do!"

Fairmind objected. "Tried everything? I doubt that. It seems to me our policy is to pretend we are trying for peace while we prepare openly and aggressively for war."

Swiftclaw ignored the other Nurturer. "They have refused to heed all our warnings! They build their forces . . ."

"In response to ours!" another Nurturer burst out. Swiftclaw threw it a baleful glance and a snarl.

"I say now is the time to act, before our enemy grows too strong and they attack us!"

"They are cubs and Chasers and Catchers and Nurturers, just as we are! Would you slaughter them?"

"Before they slaughter us!"

"What makes you think . . ." Everyone began to yell and growl at everyone else. Order dissolved into a noisy chaos. When Swiftclaw's supporters arrived, they had no trouble in quelling those who tried to put up a fight.

Are we more evil, then, than other races?

No. You're about on the norm. Of course as carnivores, you had a natural killing instinct. But even herbivores have been known to kill each other during mating battles. And in all honesty, once they become sapient, they are every bit as dangerous as carnivores. Do you wish to go on?

No, Seeker said. I've seen enough to know. This is all from what I already knew, from what I had been taught in the underground city beneath Home. It is what we are, what I am. There is no hope, then. Only despair.

If you wish it that way, it will be so.

But despair seems to be the only way out. If we admitted to despair, perhaps we could work our way to something more positive. We had so much possibility, so much potential . . .

And you never actualized it. Yes, that leads to despair, the voice said. And there were those who transcended despair and committed themselves to actuality. They went beyond possibility and actually became something. They opened themselves to one another and took infinite interest in something other than themselves. They stood revealed as what they were.

Like Grizzlebeard?

Yes, like Grizzlebeard. And thousands of others.

What did they accomplish?

They built a mighty civilization, the voice declared.

But one that destroyed itself, Seeker replied.

Yes, the voice responded, because they stopped in their actuality. They transcended despair to become real. They supported each other and created a civilization. But they still face the ultimate futility of death. It was better than before, back when they had been limited each to their individual possibility and to nothing beyond it. At least when they had committed themselves infinitely to each other, something lived on beyond them. They were born into a world they had created and it lived on after them. It was immortality of a sort. But it wasn't enough. They had to go further.

As H*mb*l has?

Yes, the voice said, as H*mb*l has. H*mb*l has leapt into the abyss with no hope of ever finding its footing again. It has infinitely resigned itself and given up all hope for the here and now. It dances only to dance and gives everything else up as lost.

But that isn't the answer either, is it? Seeker half asked, half protested. H*mb*l dances but can never be a Questioner. The hummer has gone beyond its previous actuality by infinitely resigning itself. Now it is pure potential again, pure floating in the abyss, as you said. It dances, but it dances to the rhythms of something else.

You are beginning to understand, Seeker, the voice said. H*mb*l has passed beyond one actuality into a second possibility. But it has not been able to make a final leap into a second and higher actuality.

And that actuality is a Questioner? Seeker asked.

Yes, the voice answered. And the leap that must take place is one out of the infinite and back into the finite, out of the eternity of resignation into the everydayness of existence. But the coming back into the world changes everything, turns the world inside out.

I don't know how to make that leap! Seeker wailed. I don't have the strength!

No one does, the voice whispered. Everyone does. Leap, Seeker, leap. Give up hope, give up trying, leap, and hold fast to hope and strive with all your might. Only the absurd makes sense when the world is turned inside out. Leap!

I can't . . . I can't . . . I . . .

II.

Seeker opened its eyes and looked around. It was sitting on the plain. The sun was setting behind its left shoulder. Its shadow stretched out in front of it, yearning out toward the place where the plain reached up to touch the sky.

Which plain am I on? it wondered briefly. Or does it even matter any more? Perhaps I never left the original plain there in the Reserve. Perhaps there never was a Reserve and I am sitting on the plain of Home. Perhaps I am insane, sitting in a room in the underground city staring blankly at a blank wall.

It makes no difference, Seeker realized. The problem is still the same. I must make the leap, must let go utterly, must become unsane. Wherever I am, that is the task that faces me.

And when I do, when I leap, where will I land? In Sanctuary? Or will I fall forever?

Does it really matter? If I am sitting on the plain on Labyrinth, my only hope, and that is no hope at all, is to leap. If I am still in the Reserve, my only hope is to leap. If I am sitting on the plain of Home, there is only the leap. And if I am truly in a room in the underground city, then the leap is the only thing worth trying. It has always been there, always been waiting to be made.

Seeker stood and gazed out into the distance. In the dying light the plain was incredibly beautiful. Small white flowers grew in profusion around its feet. It's the White Grass Season, the ursoid thought. I love that season most of all. I remember how the flowers stretched off into the distance, how . . .

It looked at the sun, almost gone now, just a tiny slice resting tiredly on the horizon. When the dark comes, I will leap, it decided. Leap into the night, the emptiness, the brightness, the fullness.

There is no other way.

It sighed profoundly. Slowly, slowly, the last light leaked from the horizon and the night swept in victory from the east, from where the plain rose into the sky . . .

Seeker leapt.

But to be able to come down in such a way that instantaneously one seems to stand and to walk, to change the leap into life into walking, absolutely to express the sublime in the pedestrian . . .

Soren Kierkegaard

The figure approached the odd collection of dwellings that clung to the hill. The path was dusty and no one had been along it for a long time. At the bottom of the hill it spied a building that was slightly taller than the others. It knew the one it sought would be there for sure.

It stopped in front of the building and sat down to wait. It had all the time in the world. And all the world in the time. Eventually a shadow stirred in the doorway of the building and the Pretender lifted its eyes.

"So," the shadowed figure said as it came into the light, "you found it, eh? Well, well, I won't pretend I'm not a little surprised. And a little pleased, too."

Seeker grinned. "So it was here all the time, Longarm?"

The Teacher hooted a raucous laugh. "Yes! Start and Sanctuary! One and the same! The only difference is in you. While you were a Pretender, it was Start. Now that you're a Novice, it's Sanctuary! Ha! Neat and economical, eh?"

"And you, you're part of Labyrinth, aren't you?"

Longarm grinned and nodded. "Yes. And now, so are you. I told you the planet had a way of getting into your head, didn't I? Ha! Well, I meant it, but not quite the way you thought."

"So Questioners are Labyrinth?"

"In a way. The planet can't be everywhere at once, so it uses the Questioners to be where it can't be."

"Why?"

Longarm laughed heartily. "Ah, Seeker, Seeker, made the leap and still the same! Asking questions all the time! Well, well, it's to be expected. You want to know why, eh? Well, let me hazard a guess.

"Hmmmm. Did you ever wonder where sentience came from, eh? Do you suppose it's just a natural process, an inevitable one, something that automatically takes place wherever the right molecules get together for a party?

"Well, could be, could be. But what if sentience is much rarer than that? What if it's the rarest thing in the universe? Eh, what then? Of course, you say, that can't be, Teacher. There are sentient species on many planets all throughout the galaxy. Why, you say, sentience is almost as common as arachnids.

"But what if it's true despite what seems to be the case? What if sentience has only arisen naturally once in the entire history of the galaxy? And what if that once took place not on a limited scale, like in a bunch of ursoids or simians or sauroids, but on a much vaster scale, a planetwide scale? Eh, what then?

"Can you imagine how lonely such a sentience would be? And if you were that sentience, what would you do? Eh? Easy enough to figure out. Create more sentience. Go around and give the natural processes a little nudge here, a slight push there, and ta-dah! you're not alone any more!

"But what if something goes wrong all the time? What if the sentience you help get started is always much more limited than you are? What if it only appears in a single species here and another there, but never in a whole planet? Eh?"

Longarm sighed. "A lot of 'what-ifs.' I've asked Labyrinth about it several times. Either it doesn't understand the question or it just won't answer. I told you it has been around for longer than anyone can reckon and that where it is now isn't where it came from originally. It's had plenty of time to wander all over the galaxy, Seeker. Perhaps even from one galaxy to another. To wander all over and do all kinds of things."

"And now it sends us out to keep track of its creations?" the ursoid asked, it's voice filled with wonder.

Longarm shrugged. "Maybe. Maybe not. It's only a guess. What does it matter anyway?"

"It doesn't matter at all," said a voice from behind Seeker. The ursoid turned to see Bilrog. The Furmorian warrior was smiling broadly, its sharp teeth glinting in the sunlight. "Two out of five," Bilrog announced with a chuckle. "That's better than the advertised odds."

"A miracle, at that!" Longarm declared, throwing its hands up in mock despair. "I've never seen a more unlikely lot of Pretenders in all my years as a Teacher! I . . ."

"How many of us were real?" Seeker asked.

The Teacher blinked. "Real?"

"Seeker always suspected some of us were just constructs set up by Labyrinth," Bilrog explained.

Longarm nearly choked with laughter. "Fake Pretenders? What a wonderful idea! The whole batch fakes just to try one real one? Oh, Seeker, that's wonderful!" The Teacher rocked from side to side, bent over with hilarity.

Seeker stood calmly and watched until Longarm had calmed down. "How many of us were real?" the ursoid asked again, its voice quiet but firm.

Longarm stopped laughing and stared at Seeker. Then it sighed and shook its head. "I don't know. Perhaps none of us are."

Repetition

No, in possibility all things are equally possible,
and whoever has truly been brought up by possibil-
ity has grasped the terrible as well as the joyful.

Soren Kierkegaard

I.

Redfur looked up. Its old eyes, though rheumy, were still bright with intelligence. "Eh? You again? I thought I was rid of you a long time ago. What do you want now?"

Seeker sighed. "Very little, actually. Just your permission to leave the planet. It seems such a thing must be gained before one can be allowed beyond the gate at the spaceport."

The ancient leader of the Council stared silently at Seeker for long moments. Then Redfur growled softly. "So you wish to leave the planet, eh? Might one ask why?"

"There is nothing here for me."

Redfur snorted. "How dramatic! And how trite. Nothing here for you, eh? And what's that supposed to mean?"

Seeker paused before speaking. "Well . . . technically I'm a Nurturer. On the plain, even as Slowslow the idiot, that meant something. I nurtured cubs, held them when they felt frightened or sick, sang to them, played with them."

The old Nurturer waved a paw in impatient dismissal. "Yes, yes, I know all that. We checked on you regularly. A virtual well of care and loving, you were. Stupid, but loving. Get to the point a bit more swiftly, please."

"Then I left the plain."

"Voluntarily."

"Yes. And I came back here because I remembered."

"Why come back if it was so wonderful out there?"

"There was something I was looking for. Something I had to find that wasn't there on the plain."

"Ah." Redfur sat back with a soft growl. "Now we come to it. You've been rummaging through every file in every library here on Home for years now. I know that. For a while I kept tabs on every file you read. But after a while I had better things to do, and had someone else keep tabs on you. Random nonsense."

Seeker smiled slightly. "Yes. I knew you were watching. So for several months I purposefully picked items at random to study. It wasn't until much later I really went after what I wanted. Later, even after the other you set to watch me got bored with what I was doing."

"Eh?" Redfur said, sitting forward with interest. "So you played a little trick on us. Hmmmmmm. Should have thought of that." The leader of the Council cocked its head slightly to one side. "What were you really looking for, eh?"

"The Questioner."

"Ah. The Questioner. And what did you find?"

"The truth."

Redfur was silent for several moments. "The truth? And what might that be?"

"That the Reserve was not the Questioner's idea at all. At least not in the way it was done."

"Ah," Redfur said softly. "And what was the Questioner's idea, in its pure form?"

"That we should all return to the old way, to the plain. It wasn't meant to be an experiment where a few controlled many and manipulated and changed them. The Questioner wanted us all, everyone, to start again at the beginning, to try once more, but this time with the knowledge of the mistakes we had made."

"Yes," Redfur said bitterly, "that's what the damned Questioner wanted. It wanted to turn us back into primitive savages, back into ignorant beasts that wandered the plain again." The old Nurturer's voice began to rise with anger. "It wanted us to give up all we had accomplished, all our science and technology, all our power, and become cubs again! It wanted us to move backwards into a past we had already grown out of! Not forwards, backwards!"

"And we rejected its Solution."

"Yes. The Council of that time rejected the Solution after a long and intense debate. They had to! Anything else would have been racial suicide! But we learned from what the Questioner said. Oh, yes, we learned and came up with a better plan! We created the Project!"

"To change ourselves. To become our own makers and change ourselves into what we thought was right."

"Yes! The idea of constructing the Reserve and returning part of the race to the original conditions was a brilliant concept! It allowed us a perfect opportunity to find which primitive traits were the destructive ones that had to be weeded out. You, for example, with your damed high K factor, should never have been allowed to breed. We've checked on the cubs that came from your protoeggs and destroyed them all. Every damn one of them had the same high K factor."

Seeker sat quietly for several seconds, then gave a high, keening, mournful howl. "All? All my cubs?"

"Most of your protoeggs were no good anyway, since we forced you to quick maturity with drugs. That damn fool Greyback thought you'd calm down once you were a Catcher. Ha! High K factors never settle down. We should have terminated you."

The two sat in tense silence, glaring at each other. Finally Seeker spoke softly. "You are guilty of great evil."

"I regret nothing I have done. Everything has been to save our race, to bring back the might and power we once possessed. You have seen the records. You know what we were."

"We were fools. We nearly destroyed ourselves. Our power was used for suicidal purposes."

"We made mistakes. This time we will make none."

Seeker sighed deeply. "The premise you start from is flawed, so the conclusion you reach will be equally imperfect. You take too much on yourself. You would have us be Gods to ourselves. That cannot be."

Redfur snarled. "It's you and your kind who are the fools! Fools who must be destroyed to purify our race of its weakness! You say our basic premise is flawed? I deny that!

You may not agree with it, but it is not flawed for that reason."

"No, it is not flawed for that reason. There is another reason, a far more powerful one."

Redfur stiffened and stared at Seeker with sudden apprehension. "You . . . you couldn't have found that! All reference to it was destroyed many, many generations ago! The only way it is still known is because it passes by word of mouth from Council leader to Council leader. You can't know that!"

"Yet I know. One tiny reference to it remained, hidden for many generations. I discovered it. And I have sown it once more throughout the records."

Redfur sat back, stunned and gasping for breath. "You . . . you didn't do that! No. You can't know . . ."

"But I do. I do know that when the Questioner made its report, the Council of that time was so angry it killed the Questioner. I know that the whole tale of the Solution and the Reserve, all of it, was made up to justify the Project hatched by that Council and carried on until this very moment."

The leader of the Council sat very still for several minutes, staring intently at Seeker. Finally it spoke softly. "I could have you killed."

Seeker smiled. "Yes. But you won't."

"Why?"

"Because, as I said, I have sown the information of the murder of the Questioner throughout the records. I'm the only one who knows where it is. If you kill me you might find a few of the references. But you'd never get them all in time. Nurturers would begin to find them and it would be all over for you and your damned Project."

Redfur nodded slowly, its expression grim. "Very clever. What do you want?"

"I've already told you. I want to leave the planet. There's nothing here for me any more. I know what happened, what is happening. I even think I can see what will happen. There is nothing I can do. Except leave."

"Yes, that would be best for all concerned. And in exchange you will tell me where you seeded the information of the murder of the Questioner?"

"Yes."

Redfur smiled coldly. "You are no better than we are."

"Probably not. But I only manipulate you, while you

manipulate millions. You are taking our race toward a new doom, Redfur."

The old Nurturer growled with anger. "Fool. You know nothing. Where will you go when you leave this planet? What is there for you in the galaxy?"

"Where will I go? Ah, I've thought long and hard about that one. There is only one place to go. I must complete the circle started so long ago."

"Be clear."

"I'm going to Labyrinth, Redfur. I'm going to become a Questioner."